Indentured

by

Dave McDonald

Cover design and art by Gina Mancini

Dedicated to
Mike and Cathy Giblin
for their friendship and inspiration

Chapter One

The Year of Our Lord, 1756,
Somewhere in the western Atlantic Ocean

Light streamed in from the opened hatch as did the blessing of fresh air.

Someone had kicked my leg, waking me, tugging me back to cruel reality. Over one-hundred people stuffed into this ship's hold for the past fifty-nine days. Conditions had worsened with time from bad food, minimal water, and soiled cramped bodies.

I had thought the constant motion of the ship would drive me crazy until we experienced our first violent storm. Old Mrs. Jones had been crushed to death and many others injured. The vision of Mrs. Jones' mangled, bleeding body returned every time a strong wind came up or the daytime skies darkened.

We were all passengers, many indentured servants like me, venturing to the New World. But the horrid circumstances had turned most of us into near-animals. We clung to our space and sanity.

I stretched as best I could.

I had no idea what time of day it was. Sleep had become a means of escape versus a time for rest at night.

However, I did know the exact duration of our plight for I had notched the planking daily with my knife. Today would be April fifteenth, our sixtieth day crammed in this vessel. God save me.

My head rocked back and forth on my burlap sack with the endless movement of the ship. The bag contained my few possessions, links to a life lost.

After only a few long sea-sick days into this voyage, I'd wished I'd chosen a different destination, a closer place like Europe as a location to hide and hopefully start a new life. But I'd thought distance would keep the law as well as any avenging kin from finding me and maybe help me leave my old life behind.

Unfortunately, horrible memories could neither be erased nor shared.

My eyes closed again.

My mind returned to why I was here, why I was on this God-awful ship. The vision of the child's blank eyes returned; the same eyes that haunted so many of my nights since leaving home.

My attempt at putting an ocean between me and my past hadn't worked. I feared this horrible memory was going to be my burden to carry for the rest of my life.

"Mister Hamish, Mister Hamish are you awake?" a young voice asked as a hand touched my leg.

I opened my eyelids to see a child's eyes close to mine, staring at me. I jerked up into a sitting position pressing my back against the ship's hull.

"Mister Hamish, it's me, Miles."

The second gulp of air settled me. A young, filthy twelve-year-old boy stood before me; Miles, one of my few sources of joy on this boat. "Aye, Miles." I cleared my throat. "I . . . how often do I need to tell you my name is Hamish MacCardle?"

Miles's head dropped.

I patted his shoulder. "We're long time friends, aye?"

His eyes returned to mine, and he nodded.

I smiled and gently squeezed his arm. "Aye. Then call me Hamish."

"Yes, Mr. Hamish."

I chuckled, raising my arms in surrender. "Miles, what can I do for you?"

"Me and the other kids are anxious to play one of your games. How about hide the shoe?"

I rolled my eyes. "Probably not that game. Remember the last time when one of you hid the shoe behind the chamber pot? I'll never forget Mrs. Haversham's scream when Jacob pushed the curtain aside."

Miles nodded as he giggled.

Small fingers tugged on my grimy shirt. "Com'on, Mr. Hamish, let's play," little Katy, another smile-maker, implored as the other children wedged their way into view.

The only way I kept my mind from dwelling on the squalor was to make up games to play with the dozen children trapped like me.

I pushed up on my knees as they surrounded me. Little hands patted me, little arms entwined mine, and little faces smiled, several missing teeth. My heart sang. They gave me purpose, joyful purpose.

"Give me a minute to get my mind working." A moment of fidgety kids later, I clapped my hands. "I've got one . . . a new one." I stood.

They jumped up and down and cheered.

But over the children's din, in the background from the opened hatch above us, a male voice bellowed, "Land ho!'

Without thinking I bolted over and around the kids, through the throng, and up the steps two at a time. Though we weren't allowed on deck but once a day at the Captain's bidding, I was there. Thinking it was one of my games, all the kids filed onto the deck behind me like a colony of ants after spilled sorghum.

But none of the crew was looking at us, they were all gazing forward.

I scanned our bow and there on the gray horizon was land stretching in both directions as far as I could see.

Land! Oh my God, I'd finally be getting off this always rolling and rocking, cramped, foul ship from hell. Praise be the Lord.

A deckhand approached with a scowl on his grizzled face. He was almost as tall as me. When compared to most, I was tall. He pressed close, blocking my view and motioned me below. There was no way I was going back in that hold. No way.

When I didn't move, a look of excitement flashed across the lengthy but thin deckhand's face. He inched closer, smelling of old socks. One of his hands wrapped around the handle of a rigging knife in a sheath in his rope-tied waistline.

I knew that look. Old memories flashed, horrible memories. I fisted one hand as the other found my *sgian-dubh*, the Scottish knife my father had given me before he'd left us.

"Leave that tall young man and the kids be, Smittie", the Captain ordered. "Just see them to the foredeck where they'll be out of the way."

It wasn't until I was standing on the bow of the boat that I realized it was raining. I didn't care. The sky was totally cloud-covered dimming the light. All that mattered was we had found the New World. My life was about to change, and although I had been told by so many since starting this venture how Indentured servants were treated like slaves in the New World, anything had to be better than this ship.

I didn't want to be poor like my parents.

Twelve years of labor had taught me a great trade.

With a new start, I could possibly open my own business. With a little luck, I'd earn a comfortable income as well as respect.

Though I'd ran away to save my freedom, if I had to go through seven years of servitude, so be it. I was young; twenty-two years. As long as afterwards I could achieve what I wanted.

My eyes roved over the land in the distance. All I had was hope, hope for a new future, a better life.

Chapter Two

Surrounded by the cheering and pointing children on the foredeck, I watched as our ship sailed into a large bay with a wide river emptying into it. And then in the distance I saw through the spitting rain several moored ships and beyond them a few houses. I wondered if we had reached our destination.

"Son, take the children below and tell everyone to get their possessions together," the tall Captain said to me. "By morning, we'll be docking in Philadelphia."

Below decks I conveyed the Captain's message and then in the ensuing melee sorted through my bagged belongings. I found the package from Mister Hans Blekkink. Whenever I touched his letter, I wondered what Blekkink was like? Though his written words seemed kind, would he treat me like a slave? Seven years was a long time.

"Mr. Hamish, ah, I mean Hamish, what is that?" Miles asked from over my shoulder.

I glanced at the lad and then patted the package. "It's a letter from the man who has paid for my trip to Lancaster Town in the Province of Pennsylvania."

"Really?" The skinny boy scratched his head. "Why did he do that?"

I pivoted in my squatted position to face Miles. "I agreed to work for him for the next seven years."

"So he's going to pay you?"

"Sort of, he'll give me a room, and feed me and clothe me."

Miles nodded. "Is he a friend of yours?"

I looked through squinted eyes up and away. "No. I've never met him."

Miles' eyes enlarged. "You have traveled all this way to work for someone for seven years that you don't know?"

It was my turn to nod, and my eyebrows arched, mirroring his enlarged eyes.

"Why?"

I knelt onto a knee. I so wanted to tell someone my story, anyone, even a child, but I couldn't. I closed my eyes trying to gather my thoughts but only the guilt and pain came to mind.

"Hamish?" the boy asked causing me to open my eyes.

I had to tell him something, and I didn't want to lie.

"When I was just a little younger than you, my father left us to go to England to find work. Since I was the oldest, I had to quit school and go to work."

"That had to be hard," Miles said.

"Providence smiled upon me. I got a job working as a helper for a master gunsmith in Aberdeen, a Mister

Roderick MacDonald. At first, all I did was clean and fetch whatever he needed. He paid me little, but little was better than what my family had. After several months, I don't know why, but ol' man MacDonald started testing my skills. By my fourteenth birthday, he had made me an apprentice."

"What happened to your father?" Miles asked.

I sighed. "We never heard from him. However, between what jobs my mom could find and my pay, our family struggled but survived. After seven more years of long days filled with hard work, MacDonald made me a journeyman gunsmith."

"What's that?"

"A person who is qualified to make guns. And then I made enough money that my mother no longer needed to work so hard and so often."

"So why are you here?" Miles asked.

The question that was always asked but never answered. I glanced away searching for words.

"My father returned. And . . . well, it was my time to leave. At the town center one day I saw postings from businessmen in the New World looking for help. One was from a master gunsmith named Blekkink. So here I am."

"Gosh almighty, do you really know how to make pistols and muskets?" Miles eyes got even bigger than before.

"Aye," I said, sitting a little taller. As I pulled the letter out of the package, a key fell to the floor.

"What's that for?" the inquisitive boy asked.

I picked up the key and turned it back and forth in my fingers. "I don't know. All I know is that Mr. Blekkink, the man I'm going to work for, told me not to lose it."

With the next day slipping into evening, me and my young friends stood on the foredeck again and watched as cabins, gardens, and orchards slid by on both sides of the very wide waterway. We passed numerous other vessels sailing in the opposite direction.

In the distance were the confluence of two rivers. A few miles north of the split a large city appeared on the bank. The town was like a lake of roofs bordered by wooded hills. In size it reminded me of Aberdeen. Block after block of buildings faced the water, interspersed by cobblestone streets bordered by a path of flat stones for foot passengers. And like Aberdeen, there was a man lighting street lamps as the sun kissed the horizon.

"Philadelphia!" shouted the Captain.

The children cheered and jumped up and down. At last, we'd all soon be back on land.

More passengers, humped with baggage, clambered onto the deck from the hold as our ship eased into a wharf.

I stood on sea-swaying legs on the dock in Philadelphia. I hoped that sensation would pass soon.

An old woman from the hold who the children called Esther came over to me.

"Hamish, you are indentured aren't you?"

"Ay," I said.

"Well where is your Master? All of ours are here waiting for us. Look around, all the indentured passengers are gathered on the dock with their masters."

I glanced around. "I'm supposed to meet him in Lancaster Town," I said.

She gasped. "What?" She took a step back. Then she nodded and giggled. "Oh, I see, he sent someone to get you."

"No. But he arranged for my travel there, to Lancaster Town."

Her eyes enlarged. "You are teasing me; aren't you. I know, this is one of your kids' games."

"This isn't a game, Esther. I'm supposed to stay at the Coach Inn until travel arrangements are made."

"You're not. That's where my Master stayed. Ask him, he's over there instructing one of his other servants in how to pack the wagon he brought for us to ride in." She pointed. "Over there by that fancy coach of his."

I looked and nodded. "All I know is the Coach Inn that *is* where I'm staying."

"Do you know your master?"

"No. I've never seen him."

She folded her arms and tilted her head. "And this man, after paying your ship's passage, is trusting you to come all the way to Lancaster by yourself?"

I shrugged. "Yes."

"Aren't you a gun maker?"

"A journeyman gunsmith, yes."

"So are you going to New York or Boston? I'm sure a journeyman gunsmith could get a great job in either of those towns. And you'd be free. No seven-year sentence to serve." She touched my arm. "I'm so jealous."

I shook my head. "I'm going to Lancaster. I gave my word."

She laughed so hard she rocked back and forth. Before she could reply I was surrounded by all the boat children; my friends.

Though now somewhat concerned about the prospects of my new life, I found it harder than I thought it would be to say good-bye to all those kids. We had become a mutual life-line to one and other. It was almost as bad as when I said good-bye to my mom and dad; knowing I'd never see them again. Except this time, I was able to block my tears as we separated. After all I was a man now, alone and on my own in the New World.

Although I had read Mister Blekkink's letter enough to know it by heart, I read it again. Despite this horrible boat trip, just as I'd told Esther, he had thoughtfully arranged for me to stay in a Philadelphia boarding house, the Coach Inn. I'd stay by myself until travel arrangements could be made to Lancaster Town.

Hopefully I'd be able to bath and change clothes for the first time in months. Bathing had been something I rarely had to do, and never wanted to do; until now.

After asking some locals for directions, now on more land-based legs, I found the Coach Inn. The inn was only a block off the dock. It was a wooden two-story building with a peaked clay-shingled roof and many windows. The inn consumed half of the block.

I stood in front of the large building on a lighted sidewalk. I tried to remember what a bed felt like.

As I entered the lobby lugging my burlap bag, I passed several people each of whom hesitated and looked at me like I didn't belong there.

It was only then that I realized how filthy I must look and how awful I must smell.

My first reaction was to slink into a corner, but then a thought erupted. I was Hamish MacCardle, a journeyman gunsmith, a rare commodity as my prior Scottish employer and mentor ol' man MacDonald always told me.

I squared up my shoulders and walked tall to a high desk manned by a man with a moustache and a monocle pinched between a brow and his cheek. He was dressed in a suit as if he were going to church. Was it Sunday?

I dropped my bag to the floor and slapped the counter with my palm. "I be Hamish MacCardle, and I am expected."

The man flinched. Looking up, he eyed me, then recoiled either from my height or my apparent stench. Then he tried to conceal his disgust for fear of further aggravating me.

He opened a large book and nervously thumbed through the pages and then stopped, looking up at me with a slight look of surprise. "That you are, Mr. MacCardle. The honorable master gunsmith Hans Blekkink, the Lancaster arms manufacturer, has endorsed you, and quite handsomely. Do you have a letter?"

"I do," I said, sliding the letter across the counter.

The man scanned the paper through his eye-captured monocle. Then he turned and retrieved a key. "We have a room for you, sir, one of our best. And Mister Blekkink also sent a package for you. I'll have it delivered to your room." Sliding the letter back to me, he tilted his head. "A bath has also been paid for, would you like one?"

I just nodded, fighting back a grin. I knew enough to know this wasn't how servants were treated.

I *was* somebody in this New World.

Chapter Three

I walked into my room at the Coach Inn and staggered back into the door, closing it. I had read books that described rooms like this; homes of the aristocracy.

The room was larger than my family's entire home in Aberdeen.

The four-posted-bed could have accommodated me and my three brothers and sisters. The mattress was large and sat high off the floor; tempting me to run and dive into what appeared to be a sea of softness.

The windows had ornate red curtains like nothing I'd ever seen before, with tassels.

There was a gray rug on the floor with multiple-colored-flowers woven into the border; like real flowers.

A three-person brown settee sat facing a large fireplace. I kicked off my dirty shoes and rushed over on the plush carpet to the sofa and touched a cushion. It was made of a material softer than my momma's cheek. I wanted to plop down but my clothes were disgusting. Later after my bath and a change of clothes.

No, this wasn't how servants were treated.

I wondered if I could get my bagged clothes washed? They weren't much cleaner than what I was wearing.

I stepped back, afraid to touch anything else for fear of tainting the beauty with my dirt and smell. I was standing in the middle of the room, frozen like a hungry, clumsy man holding a bucket of fresh hens' eggs, when a knock sounded at the door.

Chapter Four

A young man, about my age, stood in the doorway to my room. He was dressed in an ill-fitting uniform and cradled a large wooden chest in his arms. "Here is your package, sir."

I stared at the finely crafted wooden chest bound by leather straps and handles.

The boy grunted.

"Oh, please bring it in," I said moving aside, tingling all over. In my entire life, no one had ever given me anything with the exception of hand-made clothing from my mom, used shoes, and once a whittled wooden soldier from my dad at Christmas.

I couldn't wait to open the trunk and see if there was anything inside. But even if the chest were empty it was so much nicer than my burlap bag. However, the way the kid strained it had to be full.

He sat the trunk on the floor with a thud and hesitated, staring at me.

"Thank you," I said, my anxiety for him to leave conquered by my mother's teachings.

He squinted. "The boys are bringing you your bath." Then he spun on his toes, and took his leave.

I bolted to the chest and dropped to a knee. I tugged at the latch, but it didn't budge. Then I noticed the key hole. It was locked. The mysterious key Mr. Blekkink had sent now had a purpose. Scampering on toes and hands across the floor, I retrieved my old bag and spewed the contents on the wooden entryway floor.

My fingers fumbled inside the package containing the letter and found the key. Then I dove back to the chest. I inserted the key into the lock, and it seemed to fit.

I sat up and took a long breath trying to settle my racing heart.

My shaking fingers turned the key, and it rotated smoothly making a clacking noise. I tugged on the latch, and it flipped up.

I licked my lips and swallowed hard.

My fingers lifted the lid hinged by its leather straps.

A smell of freshness, newness, permeated my nose. A heavy tan cloth covered the brimming contents. I tugged at the thick cloth, and it unfolded becoming a thigh-length coat. Under the coat were two folded bloused-sleeve white shirts. Next was a black waistcoat, followed by a pair of dark gray breeches along with another tan pair. Beneath them was two pair of white stockings, a white cravat, two pair of undergarments, a black tricorne hat, and new leather shoes.

Unbelievable.

I leaned back and realized I hadn't been breathing. I sucked in a large breath.

Maybe this place wasn't Philadelphia, maybe I was in Heaven.

I held each item up, and they each seemed to be my size, though I was sure I was thinner than when I started.

The ship's food portions had become smaller and smaller. Lesser amounts of more and more unpalatable slop in the final weeks. And the foul food didn't stay with you long.

Now I understood why Mister Blekkink's original offer required the responders to fill in physical details.

With my heart still pounding in my ears, I continued my exploration of the chest.

I retrieved a roll of muslin next to the shoes. I unrolled it exposing a hair brush, a razor, and a black tie-ribbon for my unruly hair; like the gentlemen wore.

One thing was sure, I wasn't going to be a slave.

Underneath the muslin and shoes at the bottom of the chest was another package. I lifted it, and it was heavy and made a clinking sound.

I untied the flap and pulled out a bulging draw-string-tied bag and another letter.

I opened the bag and spilled dozens and dozens of silver and copper Spanish coins onto the floor. I retrieved and sorted the money. There was one English pound note, sixty silver shilling coins, and sixty copper pence coins. That totaled to four and a quarter pounds. More than I made in a month working for ol' man MacDonald as a gunsmith journeyman for the past year.

This Blekkink man was both generous and trustful. New clothes and enough money to at least explore a little of this New World.

Esther's words made me pause. I could run away and get lost in this vast country. With my skills, I could always find a job and never serve a day of my seven-year commitment.

I shook my head; I'd signed an agreement.

Then something glinted in the light of the room, something in a leather pocket attached to the side of the chest. I reached in and found two matching flint-lock pistols, a powder horn, and a bag of balls and paper wadding for wrapping the balls.

The pistols had Hans Blekkink's initials brass-inlaid in the mahogany handles. And the balance of the weapons was identical as well as excellent. Mr. Blekkink had skills.

All gun makers tested their products over and over; so I had become a very good marksman with both pistols and long muskets. I so wanted to fire these lovely pieces.

I now had everything I needed to flee from a long term commitment; everything but a lack of conscience.

I pondered the weapons. Blekkink's addition of the pistols made me wonder about my trip to Lancaster.

Were all the stories of the New World being filled with red savages who ate white people really true? Need I be on guard? I had only shot targets and small game, but never even thought of shooting a human being. This could be a test I didn't want to take.

I'd talk to the locals in Philadelphia about the dangers of the trip before leaving.

Running was still an option. If I could flee from this obviously caring, generous man, it'd have to be east, towards civilization.

After putting the money back in it's bag, I weighed it in my hand. Keeping my word was ingrained deep inside of me; shielded from compromise.

I would not run.

I broke his wax seal and read his letter.

Dear Mr. MacCardle,

Since you are reading this you have arrived in Philadelphia and found the Coach Inn; very well.

I anxiously await your services. My business can greatly profit from the addition of a journeyman gunsmith. Your room has been prepared here as well as a station at my company.

After you have rested, please talk to the Inn's manager. He will arrange for a coach to bring you to Lancaster along the Great Conestoga Road, a two to three-day trip. Your passage has been paid for as has your stay at the inn.

To find me, just ask anyone you see in Lancaster. Compared to Philadelphia it is a small community, just over fifteen-hundred souls, and everyone knows me.

Based on your sizes, I will be looking for a rather tall, young man.

I anxiously await your arrival,
Respectfully,
Hans Blekkink

Note: The money is yours, considerate it part of our agreement to transport you here.

The pistols are a loan. Just to ensure your safety. Though relatively few, there are ominous people in Philadelphia. Also we are currently at war with the French and Indians with several of the local tribes allying with the French. There have been a few incidents recently where travelers have been attacked. So be alert on your trip to Lancaster.

What had I got myself into?

I touched one of the ornate pistols.

This man both wanted me and was concerned about me; me.

I owed this man.

I'd come this far I must go on.

I stood. It was time for a bath, a shave, and a change of clothes. I needed to see the inn's manager and make travel arrangements.

I aimed one of the pistols. Before I ventured into the wilderness, I'd fire a few rounds with these weapons to get used to their balance and accuracy.

Chapter Five

Two days later, I stood in front of the Coach Inn wearing some of my new clothes. My sea-legs were finally gone. I had seen most of Philadelphia, drank a few tankards of grog, and shattered a few pine cones at twenty feet with the pistols.

My old clothes were washed and packed in my new trunk at my feet. An older couple also with trunks stood there awaiting the coach. Within minutes more people approached with baggage, a couple with a young son.

I couldn't take my eyes off the boy, he looked to be about ten-years-old. My stomach grumbled. Lancaster had to be at least a two-day trip. I couldn't do this. The torment would be too much. Was this God's way of punishing me?

Close to the scheduled time, a four-horse drawn coach arrived. Two men sat on a high-mounted seat. The one not driving climbed down and began tossing the luggage up to the driver where he stowed the baggage on the roof.

"Pardon me," I called up to the driver. "When is the next coach to Lancaster?"

"Three days," the man said, stopping his stacking of the luggage and staring at me. "Why, have you changed your mind about traveling with us today?"

I had enough money to stay for three more days.

The temptation to run returned. I shook the fleeing thoughts out of my head. That was no longer an option.

And I had already stayed in Philadelphia long enough. I had made a commitment to Mr. Blekkink. He was awaiting my arrival. What would I do if the next coach had a child traveling as well?

I glanced from the driver to the boy. He was just another child; no one special; he didn't even resemble anyone I knew or had known. I was out of control. Memories were in control, bad memories. In an attempt to clear my mind, I shook my head.

"No. I haven't changed my mind. I'm going with you."

After packing the luggage, the driver kneeled on the roof. "Ladies and gentlemen, before we leave, I am obligated to tell you about our journey. We will stop at Reesville for the night. We'll leave at daylight the next day for Pottsgrove for a change of horses and where two of you will disembark and others may join us. Then we'll travel to Reading where we will overnight at an inn in the fort. The next day we will travel to Lancaster. We'll stay the night, and then return to Philadelphia on the

Great Conestoga Road, a two-day trip overnighting at Exton."

Possibly two days with those young eyes looking at me. This was going to be a test.

The driver held up a musket. "My purpose is not to alarm you, and yet I must say we require all able-bodied men to bear arms during this trip. If you have none of your own, we will furnish one. There have been a few recent attacks by Indians in the area. If for some reason we are attacked, we've been told if we have many shooters the Indians will run off. So is everyone still going and how many need weapons?"

The boy's presence was no longer an issue. I had potentially much worse issues.

The other two men and the boy raised their hands.

Stomach knotted, I shook my head. With a shaking hand, I patted my old burlap bag in which I had the two loaded pistols, the powder horn, bullets, and waddings.

The thought of seeing Indians both worried and excited me. I was curious. It'd be like seeing any of the wild creatures I had heard about in Scotland that existed here. I had never seen any wild animals let alone a savage. I had done my fair share of hunting small game in Scotland, but nothing life threatening. The thought of seeing anything wild and dangerous was exciting as long as it was from a safe distance.

But what would I do if we were attacked? How would I react if a savage tried to kill me or any of us? Could I shoot an Indian? Was that any different than killing a wild animal?

They were men.

I didn't want to hurt or kill another human being; never again.

The driver held the door as the six of us climbed on board and sat where he had instructed. The men and boy at the windows and the women in the middle.

"I suggest you spend early on teaching the women how to load a musket and the boy how to shoot one," the driver glanced at the nervous women, "just in case. I doubt if we have any trouble. We never have had. But it's always wise to be prepared."

He closed the door. Within what seemed like minutes, we rolled out of Philadelphia into the wooded hills of Pennsylvania. Rocking farther and farther away from the protection of the city.

"We are the Schmidts, from New York City," the older gentleman finally broke the bouncy silence. "Emma and John. I'm a forge operator, and we're going to Pottsgrove where I've been offered a job."

We all looked at each other to see who would speak next.

"I'm George Hastings and this is my wife Martha and our son Joshua. We are going to Lancaster to my parents' farm. They are getting up in years and asked us to help them. "

Just my luck, the couple with the young boy were going to Lancaster. We'd be together the entire trip.

It was my turn to introduce myself. I had worked so hard to become a journeyman. I had made a lot of sacrifices to be here, to escape the hangman. I sat up a little taller. "I'm Hamish MacCardle," my voice cracked in the middle of my name. I cleared my throat. "I'm a journeyman gunsmith from Aberdeen, Scotland. I'm going to Lancaster to work for a master gunsmith there." These people didn't need to know I was indentured.

Mr. Schmidt smiled and leaned in and patted my knee. "You've accomplished a great deal for such a young man. Well done. I'm sure the young women of Lancaster will be happy to have such a tall, handsome young man arrive, especially one with such a promising future. We are blessed to have someone on board who is familiar with weapons. My wife and I know nothing about guns."

I shrugged. "Afraid there aren't any Indians in Scotland."

"We can be of help," George Hastings said. "Years ago, I served in the British Army and both my wife and son know how to load and shoot a musket. We're from

Albany, and yes we've had some encounters with both the French and the Indians."

"What are they like, the Indians?" I blurted without thinking about the Schmidts who were obviously as nervous as me.

"We're pushing the Indians out of their homes and off their land," George said. "How would you be?"

I thought of my youth and how I'd learned to fight for what belonged to me and my family after my dad left us. I nodded.

"The driver doesn't seem to think we'll have any problems," John Schmidt said, squeezing his wife's hand. "But just in case, would you mind showing both me and my wife how to load and use these muskets?" John Schmidt tapped the rifle braced against the side of the coach.

"I think between my wife, son, and I, along with Mr. MacCardle, we can surely do that," George said.

Just as we were finishing teaching the Schmidts how to load and shoot muskets, I glanced out the window. In a meadow there were half a dozen of the largest four-legged beasts I'd ever seen.

"What are those?" I asked pointing.

George Hastings sat forward to look out the window. "Those are what the locals call buffalo. I'm quite sure there are none in the British Isles."

"No nothing like them. Nothing. They are huge. Are they dangerous?"

"I've been told if they have calves they can become aggressive," George said. "However, they're not a meat eater."

"Like cows? Do they give milk?"

"They are similar to a cow. They're a mammal and suckle their young. I would guess they could be milked, but I wouldn't suggest trying it. Their meat is quite like beef, very edible."

"Are there any deadly animals?"

"Many," George said. "Besides the Indians, there are mountain lions, poisonous snakes and spiders, wolves, bears, and I'm sure other things I've forgotten to mention."

"May God preserve me," I exclaimed. "How do people survive?"

"They learn or . . . or else." George sat back.

"We've been told the land stretches for thousands of miles westward, with many large rivers, mountains, and deserts." John Schmidt said.

"This place is so different," I said. "It's fantastic and yet scary." I scratched my head. "I have so much to learn."

"Ask questions like you are now," George said. "Listen and learn. And be aware of your circumstances and what to look for. Stay armed and you should be fine.

However, mind you, here in the wilderness, there are no guarantees."

Chapter Six

An hour or two after the last stop to water the horses at a creek, the coach haltered again in a patch of woods on top of a nob. This stop hadn't been announced as had the others. Pistol in hand, I stuck my head out of the window. The sun was low on the western horizon.

"Charley, do you see the flag?" the driver asked. "I don't see it."

"No, me neither."

"William always puts it up, always, unless . . . unless there's a problem, and he doesn't want us to come in."

A knot formed in my stomach. I looked ahead and could see the rooftops of several houses atop the next rise, three hundred or so yards ahead. A grassy meadow filled the valley between us and the hamlet.

"What's going on?" Mr. Schmidt asked.

I held up an open hand to quiet him.

"What'll we do?" Charley asked.

"Well it'll be dark in an hour," the driver said. "We can't go back to Philly, and we can't stay here. We can turn around, bypass Reesville, and try to get to Exton before dark. And then decide whether to go from there to Pottsgrove tomorrow or to Lancaster."

"William knows me," Charley said. "Give me the musket, and you keep the Pennsylvania long rifle. I'll go check out the hamlet. If you hear a shot, or I don't come back in a half-hour turn around and head for Exton."

"Charley, you stay and I'll-"

"Give me the musket" Charley said. A moment later, he climbed down and ran down the road toward the meadow.

"Any of you good with a long gun?" the driver asked leaning down toward the coach and seeing me.

"I am," I said, in a moment of pride without thinking.

"Climb up here."

What had I done? Everyone in the coach was looking at me. I had no choice. I pocketed my gun. Shouldering my burlap bag, I got out and climbed up onto the seat next to the driver. The man was built solid with graying stubble on his chiseled face.

His green eyes scanned me. "What's your name, son?"

"Hamish, Hamish MacCardle, sir."

"Hamish, I'm going down to that meadow between us and the hamlet so I can turn this rig around,' the driver snapped the reins on the horses' backs. "Giddyup, Duke!" The coach rolled forward. "After we turn around, you get on top with that Pennsylvania long rifle and cover our rear. Just don't shoot Charley."

"I overheard what you two said," I shouted over the noise of the rig as I held onto my hat. With my other hand, I pulled the pistol out of my pocket.

The driver nodded and steered the team down the hill and into the meadow. He eased the coach off the road and turned around.

The stories I'd heard in Aberdeen claimed an Indian could hide behind a clump of grass or a small bush. My eyes scanned the grass looking for any movement as my fingers tightened around the weapon's grip.

Rolling back onto the road, the driver stopped the coach.

I climbed up on the roof. I set my handgun down as he lifted the rifle up to me. Facing the rear and straddling luggage, I laid the long gun down. I took the second loaded pistol out of my bag with shaking hands and laid it next to the other handgun on the rooftop. Then I shouldered the long musket and rested the end of the barrel on a suitcase. With fumbling fingers, I cocked the weapon and took a deep breath and eased it out.

"What's going on?" George Hastings called from inside the coach.

"Gentlemen, arm your muskets and cover the meadow on both sides of the coach," the driver said standing, holding the reins, and looking back over my shoulder. "And be quiet."

Sweat trickled down the curvature of my spine for a long silent moment.

"If there are Indians in the hamlet, how many do you think there are?" I asked softly, trying to keep both my volume and tone in control.

"There are at least a dozen people in Reesville, most with guns," the driver said. "I'd guess if the Indians came to attack the community they'd bring a lot more than a dozen. There are hundreds, maybe even thousands of Indians in this area."

"Really." I gulped. "Ah, do these Indians have guns?"

"I don't think so, unless the French gave them some. Normally all they have are bows and arrows, spears, knives, and hatchets. But they know how to use them."

"Hatchets?" I asked.

"I can imagine the stories you've had to have heard about Indians," the driver said. "Just remember, they are just men like you and me. And if anyone but a white man comes down that road or out of those woods, shoot him. Better yet, kill him."

We were no more than a hundred yards from the village. If this weapon was as good as the ones I'd made in Scotland, I could put a ball within an eight-inch circle at this distance. But could I intentionally kill another human being? The Aberdeen tales about the New World's savages returned. What if he were a screaming red man wielding a hatchet running at me to take my scalp? What if there were twenty or thirty of them or a hundred?

I took another deep breath and tried not to think.

A flock of birds erupted out of the woods up the hill near the hamlet. I gasped. Heart lurching, I jerked the gun in the direction of the birds.

And then over top of the bushes and trees on the hillside, a flag arose on a pole.

"Thanks be to God," the driver said, as he sat down on the seat, blowing out a breath. "Come down from there, son." He leaned over and yelled into the coach. "Stand down. Everything is all right."

I blinked a trail of sweat out of my eyes and slowly climbed down.

Chapter Seven

Sleeping in the barn in Reesville with the rest of the coach passengers was far better than trying to sleep on the ship. There was safety in armed numbers and the hay was soft. I slept a sound dreamless sleep.

Awoken before light, I was greeted with cool morning air and a ground fog. A light breakfast made by William's wife, Janet, was served four-at-a-time in their cabin. At first light, the eight of us boarded the coach and rolled off into the eerie fog.

By mid-morning the fog had burned off except for the low areas. The interior of the coach was quiet as the women and the boy had fallen asleep shortly after we started bouncing along the dirt road.

A mile or two after crossing a shallow stream, the coach climbed into a thick, mature woods. Between the cool air and the dim light, I was on the verge of dozing off when the coach stopped. I bolted upright and fished a pistol from my pocket, scanning the misty woods out the window.

"Gentlemen," the driver called, "I need two of you to give Charlie a hand in moving a fallen tree off the road. The remaining two need to get their weapons and cover our sides."

Mr. Hastings, rifle in hand, and I with my pistols stuffed in my coat, got out and walked forward. We were waist deep in the gray mist foot-searching for tree limbs, rocks, and holes. Fear of the unknown forced my hand to grip one of the pistols.

Charlie, carrying an axe and a musket with wound ropes over his shoulder, met us in front of the horses. Branches laden with leaves stuck up out of the dense fog across our path.

The driver tied the reins around the hand brake. Then he climbed on the roof with the long rifle in hand. "Let me know when you're finished," he said with his back to us and his head turning from side to side.

"Hold this," Charlie said as he handed me the axe. Then, musket cocked and shouldered, he waded into the fog to the base of the tree. "Looks like a lightning strike to me. It's charred at both ends of the break." He disarmed the gun.

"Good," the driver said.

"What's good about that?" I asked.

"Both robbers and Indians are known for falling trees across a known coach path," Charlie said. "This tree fell because of Mother Nature, not by man. Now give me that axe. You and Mr. Hastings tie a rope around the tree on each side of where I start chopping. After I chop through it, we'll drag the two halves off the road."

Close to twenty-minutes later, the road was clear. Charlie was climbing up to sit next to the driver. I stood along side the coach, waiting for Mr. Hastings to climb inside.

Movement caught my eye. I turned and an Indian, belly-deep in the fog, stepped out of the shadows in the woods less than five paces from me. The bare-chested copper man wore a red headband across his forehead disappearing under his long dark hair that touched his shoulders. He stood unmoving, muscular arms hung by his tapered sides. His cold dark eyes locked on mine, conveying hate. The top of his lip rose baring clenched teeth. His fierceness was accentuated by a wide scar linking his temple to his jaw.

My air was gone. My muscles useless. I just stood there, not breathing or moving; a statue. It was as if time had stopped and the two of us were captured in the void. Standing. Staring. Unmoving.

Then he was gone. Not a sound, just gone into the darkness of the dense woods.

I gasped, the sudden intake of air jolted me. My hands struggled to pull my pistols from my coat. I tried to scream a warning to the others but only a wordless groan was emitted.

"Hamish get-what the hell?" the driver exclaimed looking down over his shoulder at me.

I found myself facing the woods, both arms extended, aiming the cocked pistols at blackness. "An . . . an Indian . . . there was an Indian right in front of me a . . . a second ago."

"Get in the coach, now!" the driver screamed.

I leaped inside.

The coach rolled away, with the whip-cracking driver yelling at his lead-horse.

Chapter Eight

I spent the remaining, bone-jarring trip to Pottsgrove with a thudding heart and a dry mouth. A pistol in each hand, I checked out every tree and bush along the road for Indians.

Once before in my life a man had looked at me like that scar-faced Indian had. They both wanted to kill me. I'd understood why the other man had hated me. I'd given him just cause. But how could that red man hate me just for the color of my skin?

John Hastings' words returned. We were taking away their lands, their homes.

I didn't belong here; maybe none of us white people belonged here.

When the coach rolled into the small village on a river, exhausted from the tension, I slumped into my seat. My heart rate slowed and all I wanted to do was sleep.

"Pottsgrove, everyone out," the driver hollered. And he and Charlie began passing down the Schmidts' luggage.

"It's . . . it's not very big, John," Emma Schmidt said, eyebrows arched, glancing around.

I had to agree with her. Pottsgrove wasn't much larger than Reesville. The village had maybe fifteen or twenty homes and a large barn-like building; probably the foundry where Mr. Schmidt would work. There was no fort, no place to collect for safety and defense except the large building. And then I noticed the rifle slots in the sides of the building. That was their fort as well as their workplace. Who kept watch at night or during the day when all the men were working?

A shiver rippled through me. I wouldn't want to live here.

"Nothing is very big compared to New York City, my dear," John replied and patted her hand. "We'll be fine, Emma. A month from now you'll never want to leave."

"There's something to be said about large cities," Emma said.

"And what might that be?" John asked, putting on his hat.

"They don't get attacked by Indians," Emma said, following the boy out of the coach.

"Nice to have made your acquaintance, and I pray the lessons in firearms use doesn't come in handy," John Schmidt said to the Hastings couple and me as he climbed out.

"I pray that as well," Mrs. Hastings said as she glanced at her husband. Her eyes echoed Mrs. Schmidt's feelings.

After consuming a chunk of bread and some water, I curled up in a hay-strewn horse stall inside the foundry while the horses were being fed and watered.

"Did you hear what ol' man Johnson said to me when we exchanged horses?" I recognized Charlie's voice though I couldn't see him.

"No," the driver answered.

"He told me Mr. and Mrs. Clark were supposed to join us for the trip to Lancaster. They have a cabin a couple hundred yards into the woods. All this Indian talk had her shaking scared. They decided to start over again in Lancaster."

"Yes, I had been told others would be joining us here," the driver said.

"Well when they didn't show up this morning, Johnson and a couple of armed men went to find them. Their place was empty and everything had been either taken or torn to shreds."

"Damn," the driver said. "That poor woman."

"Nothing like this has happened around here before," Charlie said. "Maybe we should go back to Philadelphia. Maybe this is not a good time for going further west."

"These people paid us to take them to Lancaster, Charlie, and that's what we're going to do." There was a hesitation and shuffling of feet. "Keep this to yourself.

No need in frightening our passengers any more than they already are."

Footsteps thumped out of the building.

There was no way I was going to sleep now. I set up, leaning against the wall. My mind kept returning to the scarred Indian's face; over and over.

The sound of a gunshot brought me to my feet. A second shot caused me to fumble my pistols out of my coat as I stepped from the stall.

A bent, gray-haired gentleman appeared from behind a large furnace. "Easy there, son. I believe those shots are from our hunting party. Four or five of our men go out into the wilderness twice a week to find meat for the town. Our lads are good shots. We all have Pennsylvania long rifles. One to two shots are all we ever need to kill an animal. Just wait. If there are no more shots, then there is no need to be alarmed."

The older gentleman and I stepped outside. Mr. Hastings, the driver, and Charlie were there with their muskets. The old man looked at the church at the end of row of homes. A man in the bell tower waved at him.

"Everything is fine," the man said.

Releasing a held breath, I pocketed my weapons.

I wouldn't want to live here.

And yet I was going further away from civilization.

I looked to the heavens. Was living in the wilderness fearing for my life every minute my penance for what I had done in Scotland?

Chapter Nine

The coach rolled out of the small village at midday.

The driver had said before that there were hundreds of Indians in this area; maybe even thousands!

I checked both pistols to assure myself that they were primed. Though I knew the pistols were loaded and ready for use, I had to be sure. My hands shook through the process. I hadn't been this nervous since I left home.

An anxiety-filled hour or so after leaving Pottsgrove, George Hastings straightened his slender frame and broke the dusty silence. "That's the Schuylkill River we're following, the same river that runs through Pottsgrove. According to my folks, Reading is a much larger settlement than the village we just left. The town was laid out around ten years back by the sons of William Penn. There's a fort there." He squeezed his wife's hand. "We should be in Lancaster by dinner time tomorrow."

"You know a great deal about the area," I said, hoping to extend the conversation in order to distract my raving mind. "Have you been here before?"

"No. But my parents write to us often. They've been in Lancaster for close to three years. My father was an officer in the British Army and was awarded a tract of land in Lancaster when he retired from the army. Fortunately, he got out of the army before Braddock's campaign. Braddock and over two-thousand men came through here just a year ago on their way to capture the French Fort Duquesne. It was a disaster. Braddock and almost half of his men were killed."

"I had heard rumors in Scotland of the French defeating Braddock."

"It wasn't the French," Hastings said. "It was the Indians who slaughtered the British troops who were unskilled at wilderness fighting."

I recalled the evil stare of the scarred Indian in the woods. Despite the warm summer air flowing through the coach's windows, I had to suppress a shiver. I wondered if he were involved in that battle.

"My father has since found that farming in this hilly country isn't practical, however iron ore mining pays very well," Hastings continued. "He now owns several mining companies that supply tons of iron ore to the rest of the British America; particularly Lancaster." He flipped one of his hands in my direction. "As you must know, Lancaster is one of the biggest producers of weapons in the British America."

I nodded.

"Though Martha and I are farmers and my parents live on a large tract of land, we're going to Lancaster to help my parents run their mines. It will be a big change for us, but we're excited about our new life as you must be."

I pondered a treeless flat meadow, a rarity in this hill country, as it slid by the bouncing window. Then I glanced at his wife and boy before responding. "This vast country is definitely a big change for me. My success will be dependent on yours."

He smiled.

As the sun neared the tips of the hills, the coach driver announced, "Post of Reading in sight."

Relieved to be safe and soon to be out of this rocking, bouncing coach, we all smiled at each other.

Minutes passed.

"Oh, my God," Mrs. Hastings said, covering her nose with her hand.

Then I smelled it. The same disgusting odor that had permeated the ship's hold after old Mrs. Jones had been crushed to death and nothing could be done about her until the storm subsided a day later.

The smell was so vile I could taste it.

"God almighty", Charlie said from the driver's bench above us. "Why did they do that?"

"Ma'am, you and the boy need to close your eyes for a bit," the driver called down.

Mrs. Hastings motioned for her son to come sit between her and her husband. When he did, she covered his eyes with her free hand and closed her own eyelids.

I stuck my head out of the coach's window. "Oh my God," I said pulling my head inside. My stomach churned.

Roughly a half-mile from the stockade, three tall charred poles were stuck into the ground. What was left of three adult male Indians were nailed through their raised hands to each of the poles. They had been scalped and a fire had been set at their feet, burning off most of their lower legs and cooking their remaining skin. I glanced out the other side and three more charred poles came into view.

The driver whipped the horses into a trot through the cortege of barbarity.

The combination of the visual horror and the smell made me pull off my hat, lean out the window, and puke over and over until there was nothing left.

Gasping for breath I fell back into my seat.

No wonder the scarred Indian hated me and all white people.

Chapter Ten

The sun had almost finished its daily duties when our coach rolled through the opened gates of the Reading stockade. Men, women, and children emerged from tents, lean-tos, and the fort's inn, all coming to see who had arrived, or for the mail, or for just whatever verbal news they could hear.

After Mr. and Mrs. Hastings and the boy got out of the coach, I climbed down.

A man close to my height in a British uniform walked up and held the lead horse.

"In God's name, what the hell did you think you were doing out there, Ensign Biddle?" our driver said hiking his thumb over his shoulder. "You're becoming more savage than the damned Indians."

I had taken a couple of steps toward the inn, it had been a long day, but I stopped as did the Hastings. We wanted to hear this conversation.

"Frank, I will report your words to Lieutenant-Colonel Conrad Weiser," the ensign said, looking up at our driver, who was standing on top of the coach. "The lieutenant-colonel will be happy to know his message was received."

"And what message is that?" the driver asked as he handed a bag down to Charlie.

"Two days ago, our company was on patrol when we spotted smoke in the direction of George Zeisloff's place." He patted the horse's forehead. "On the way we ran into that bunch of Lenape Indians you saw out there, eight of them, we killed two in the encounter. The bastards had five fresh scalps tied to their lances. We tied the six barbarians together and dragged them to George's place. All that was left of his house and out-buildings were smoldering ashes." The ensign looked away and down. "Poor George and his wife, two young sons, and baby girl had been scalped, disemboweled, and left in the house to burn alive."

Mrs. Hastings gasped and clutched her husband and boy.

The driver stopped unloading bags and bowed his shaking head.

My stomach knotted but I had nothing left to throw up.

"George, and maybe his wife Sally, or possibly Zebadiah, his oldest boy who was ten, had killed three of those God-less creatures."

The ensign looked up at the driver with cold eyes. "And you ask what message Lieutenant-Colonel Weiser wanted to send? He wanted the remaining warring Indians to know that we can be as savage as them. And this *will* be their fate if we catch them. And believe me, their Indians brothers had to have heard their screams."

Shaking inside, I walked away wondering if we'd ever get to Lancaster alive.

As my father had always said relative to the relationship of the Scots with the Brits, 'Hate begets hate.'

This New World was overflowing with abomination.

These weren't civilized people any longer, they had become animals.

There was no way I could stay here seven years.

I had made one horrible mistake in my life, but I wasn't an animal then or now.

I didn't belong here.

What had I done?

Chapter Eleven

I'd spent a night in the Reading Stockade's inn filled with visions of screaming savages overwhelming me. The last thing I wanted to do was to get back in that damned coach and travel into a wilderness inhabited by thousands of the white-people-hating Indians.

At breakfast in the inn I overheard Ensign Biddle tell our driver we would be getting an escort of ten men to Lancaster. My first reaction was ten men had to be close to a fourth of the men garrisoned here. Someone was expecting we would be attacked between here and Lancaster. However, the thought of sixteen shooters also gave me enough assurance that I could at least eat without my hands shaking.

Despite the coach being both led and trailed by five armed, mounted-men, the Hastings and I sat in nerve-frayed silence with weapons at ready as the coach left the stockade.

With the stockade and row of gore behind us, George Hastings decided it was time to break the tension-saturated silence. "Did anyone prepare you for this . . . this place, Hamish?"

I blew out a long breath. "I had heard many horrible stories of the atrocities committed by the savages in the New World. At the time, I thought the savages were the Indians."

George bit his lower lip and slowly nodded his head. "It's frightening to witness what fear and hatred do to civilized men."

"Knowing those stories, why did you come here?" Martha Hastings asked. She sat down her musket, leaned forward, and clasped her hands over her son's ears. "If we didn't have needy kin in Lancaster," she glanced at her husband, "believe me, we wouldn't be taking this risk." Then she released her son and took up her gun.

"Precisely," George added.

I studied the little woman with the clamped jaw and the white-knuckled grip on the rifle. She had made a choice. Knowing what she knew, a very brave decision. She had taken a big risk with her life and the lives of her family while making a personal sacrifice for her husband's family. I had to admire her.

"Why did you come here?" Her words echoed in my head.

I wasn't a liar. There was no need to lie. I just couldn't tell all of my story. I was going to have to live in the same town with these people for the next seven years. "Why did I come here? Ever since we left Philadelphia, I've been asking myself that question over and over."

I cleared my throat. "In Scotland, my future had been pretty much determined. I would've had a roof over me head, food on the table, and a fire in the hearth. No Indians or wild animals to fear, just each day like the next. Growing up, I watched journeymen like me trudging to and from work. Men old for their years, with the life fading from their eyes early on."

I hesitated, rubbing my chin. "The New World sounded like a chance for a new life, a better life. Better than the one I would've had if I stayed in Scotland. What I didn't know, was how far into the wilderness Lancaster was."

George nodded and his wife rolled her eyes.

I stiffened. I thought my words were believable. Could she see through me? I released a held breath. "What's wrong?" I asked her.

"Nothing," she snapped.

"No, something is bothering you. What is it?"

"What is it, Martha?" her husband asked, causing me to wonder if she needed his consent to speak.

Her dark eyes fixed on mine causing me to wish I hadn't asked.

"You would've become a master gunsmith in Scotland. Am I correct?"

"Eventually, yes."

She nodded. "When I was a child in London, my father worked for the government. We lived well, in a very respectable neighborhood. We had servants."

She glared at George who looked away, out the window.

Obviously I wasn't the only one who had made a mistake.

"The only nicer and bigger home on our street was owned by a master gunsmith. I don't understand. Why would anyone leave that *civilized* wonderful life to come to this Godforsaken place?" Her words sliced the air between us like an on-target arrow; too fast to dodge.

I needed this job in Lancaster. I couldn't jeopardize what future I may have. I didn't know what to say to this probing woman. Needing time to think of a reply, I Eased my pistols back into my coat pockets, one at a time.

George came to my rescue. "Once we get to Lancaster we should be safe. Lancaster is quite large compared to the tiny settlements we've encountered so far. The borough is inhabited with over one-thousands souls. It has a larger stockade than Reading, and the fort is a storage and distribution center for the local gun makers' arms and ammunition. I would venture to call Lancaster civilized." He glanced at his wife.

George's words eased the knots in my shoulders. Maybe life wouldn't be so tense in Lancaster.

I glanced at Martha, and she was staring at me suspiciously.

This woman had a story she wasn't telling. And yet, she was bound and determined to find out my real story.

This wasn't over.

Chapter Twelve

Close to mid-morning, our little caravan came to a stop. I stuck my head out the window. Our lead group of soldiers had dismounted and stood at ready behind their horses with their guns aimed forward. In the distance, a group of riders were galloping toward us. I got out of the coach with pistols cocked in both shaking hands.

As the approaching men got closer they slowed to a trot. A shock of red hair bobbed into view. They were eight armed young white men. When they reined in just short of our soldiers, I could see all their features. I estimated all of them to be under the age of twenty.

"Aren't you ol' man Isiah Johnson's boy?" one of our lead soldiers asked, pointing at the red-headed boy.

"That be me," said the tall thin boy pushing a lock of red hair away from his eyes.

"What're you boys doin' on your own this far from Reading?"

"Hunting," a short, blond, stocky boy answered.

"It's a wonder any of you still have your hair!" the soldier said, shaking his head.

"Oh we've got our hair and more," the red-head boy said. "We're going to be rich. The hunting was good."

"How so?"

The blond boy reached into a bag he had tied across his chest and removed three bloody scalps. "The Pennsylvania Governor declared just the other day that the government will pay one-hundred-thirty pieces of eight for the scalp of every male Indians over the age of ten. And we have three!"

His companions cheered.

"How many were you when you started?" the soldier asked.

"Same as now, eight," the blond said, sitting a little taller in his saddle.

"How'd did you boys get close enough to kill three warriors and live to tell about it?"

"Uh . . . they weren't warriors . . . least ways not yet; they were children," the red head said lowering his eyes. Then he looked up at the soldiers with a determined expression. "But they's all over the age of ten, I swear."

My mouth dropped open as my gun holding arms fell to my sides. "Oh my God."

George Hastings stepped out of the coach. "Did I hear them correctly?"

"That fool governor is going to get us all killed," I whispered to George.

Chapter Thirteen

"Indians!" the driver yelled, within a quarter of an hour after passing the eight boys heading to Reading. "Head for those fallen trees in the meadow to the right." The whip cracked and the coach's speed increased as we left the road. The five soldiers behind us galloped past us.

Bouncing, I fumbled my pistols out of my coat. I stuck my head out the window. We were in a valley surrounded by wooded-hills. I couldn't see anything other than the ten soldiers leaping off their horses and dropping behind the logs.

The Hastings, all jostling trying to stay in their seats, had their guns pointed out of the windows and were scanning the area.

We were nearing the clump of downed-trees and the driver slowed the horses.

"There!" The boy sitting next to me pointed out his window.

I looked over his shoulder and saw twenty or thirty Indians mounted on horses gallop past us on the road. They glanced at us but keep going.

"They're going after those boys", our driver yelled. "And as fast as they're going, they'll soon catch them. Those boys won't have a chance."

"Do you want us to try to help them?" the lead soldier, a sergeant, asked.

Our driver climbed down and opened a coach door. "Folks, I can't make that decision. It's up to you. We're about halfway to Lancaster. Do you want to risk going on without an escort?"

I looked at George Hastings. "This is your decision to make George. You have your family to consider. I'll go along with whatever you decide." The knots returned to my shoulders. I prayed I wouldn't regret my words.

George looked at his wife. "If we had settled at Reading, one of those boys could've been Joshua."

"I was just thinking the same thing. Tell them to go . . . go now."

Our driver turned to the soldiers. "Sergeant, you heard the lady. God's speed and may you save those boys and yourselves."

"You heard him, men, saddle up we got some riding to do," the sergeant ordered.

The ten soldiers were mounted and gone in seconds.

I hadn't felt that alone since I boarded the ship leaving Scotland and my family.

"May God bless you, ma'am." Our driver climbed back up to his seat. "We need to make up some time,

Charley." The whip snapped, and we were jolted and jarred back toward the road.

Chapter Fourteen

No one in the coach seemed interested in talking after the military escort left us in the wilderness. We all were too busy looking for Indians. Surely they would find us and attack. We were alone, a woman, a small boy and four men. Based on what little I knew, we should be easy pickings for a war party.

The driver pushed the horses, resting only in the middle of large clearings; stopping to water them at streams where there was no cover.

The horses ran. We searched.

Squinted eyes strained, nerves peaked, especially when the coach rolled through thick woods; on and on, one dust-generating mile after another.

Just when my concentration started to lose its battle with my exhaustion, Charlie let out a "Whoop! Whoop!" He leaned down. "Lancaster Town in sight. We made it."

Lancaster Town, my new home, was a welcome sight.

On approach, the town appeared as a lake of roofs in a clearing, and looked larger than Aberdeen.

"Look, Martha, there's one of the watch towers Father said he helped build," George Hastings said.

"Watch tower?" I asked sticking my head out the window to see a wooden tower much higher than any of the homes in the town. The structure was placed in the area cleared around the town. There were several of them spaced apart in the visible area.

"Lancaster is one of the most western British towns in the British America. Being this far into the wilderness as well as into the French claimed territories, the town must have a means of defense. And since the town is growing at such a fast rate, a stockade wouldn't work. So the area around the town has been cleared and these towers built. They are manned day and night. At night fires are burned at the edge of the clearing. Each tower has a bell. If an attack does come, the bell is rung, alerting everyone in town to go to the fort."

I shook my head. "I wouldn't want to be that person in the tower if an attack comes."

"Hopefully they have time to climb down and run," George said.

The horses slowed to a walk as we rolled into the town. House after house, either wood or stone, mostly stone, lined the streets, with streets behind streets. Glancing down intersecting avenues, I could see a wide river in the distance winding along forming another border to the village.

Many of the town's people saw the coach and begin walking along beside us. Pointing at us as if we were different, they talked among themselves, some happy, some not.

George Hastings clutched his wife's hand. "We're home. Thanks be to God."

"Amen," she said. Her eyes went from her husband to me. "Hamish, after we get settled you must come for dinner one night. We can share what our new lives are like and . . . and maybe our old ones as well."

Though she smiled her eyes conveyed something other then joy, perhaps suspicion.

I nodded, but I doubted that would happen.

If given a chance, Mrs. Hastings would not quit prying until she knew my past.

Chapter Fifteen

As the sun neared the horizon, pulling the waning light trailed by darkness, the coach rolled to a stop. "We're at the Lancaster Town center," the driver said. "This is the point where arriving coaches unload. Anyone expecting you should be here. I'll toss down your luggage from Charlie's side, so please get out of the coach on my side."

Outside the coach a small group of people stood in the porch shade of a two-story building. I wondered if Mister Blekkink was one of them. I chewed on my lip, mulling over how my life could change, from better to worse.

"Have you a tall man on board, a Mister Hamish?" I heard a deep voice with a guttural accent ask.

"Yes, we do," the driver said.

I waited for the Hastings to exit the coach, and then I climbed out on unsteady legs.

A short, stocky man, who looked strong enough to pick up one of our horses, approached, wearing a black vest over a white shirt, gray breeches, and a too-small tricorne hat perched upon his massive black-haired head. "Hamish, Hamish MacCardle?" he asked as he pointed at me.

"Aye," I answered. "Mr. Blekkink?"

"Yes, that be me, laddie," the-stub-of-a-man responded. "Thank God you are here . . . and with your hair." He grasped my hand and squeezed my knuckles white. "If I had known things would have gotten this bad this quickly, I would have hired a couple of dozens men here to join me to come to Philadelphia to get you."

I pried his hand off my aching hand. I flexed my fingers to ease the pain, though his words concerning my well-being had diverted my focus.

"I cannot tell you how glad I am that you are here," Mr. Blekkink said shaking his large head. And before I could react he wrapped his stout arms around me and hugged me, raising my feet off the ground.

First my hand and now my ribs, had this man paid for me to come all this way so he could crush me to death? Though breathless, he had squeezed a smile out of me.

Finally, he set me down and let me go.

I stood bent at the waist trying to get air into my lungs.

"I cannot remember being so happy. Wait until you see the house and the shop. Your room is ready and your work station is in place. We, you and I, are going to make some fine weapons, son. Just wait and see. I have orders on top of orders. We are going to be very busy for a long time."

All I could do was nod and smile. I had never experienced such a warm welcome. He made me think I belonged here. Like I was home. Words failed me.

This short, stout man had kindled my hope. Maybe, just maybe, I could make a new life in Lancaster Town.

Chapter Sixteen

Just before the fading light slid into darkness, Hans Blekkink stopped the carriage in front of a large two-story stone house on the edge of town. From what I could see, the house had windows on all sides of the home. Behind the home was a covered well, a big garden, a small smoke house, and another large stone structure beyond which was a wooden barn. Behind the barn was the clearing that bordered the town. Several hundred feet beyond the house was one of the watch towers.

"Welcome home, Hamish," Mister Blekkink said. "My . . . our shop is behind the house. You'll be staying there, in the loft."

I glanced at the house again and noticed the first floor windows had the wooden shutters pulled closed. "Why are the first floor windows boarded up?"

"I did not want to live in the middle of town; too many people. Also, I did not want the hammering and pounding noises of my business disturbing anyone. So I built my place out here, on the periphery of the town. With the recent problems with the French and Indians, the homes on the outskirts of town have become the first line of defense. So I keep the first level boarded up. And since the house is stone, it will not burn as easily. So it is my little fort. Speaking of which, I will show you the town's fort tomorrow. You will need to know where it is."

I nodded though a brick had just been dropped in my stomach. "Doesn't your wife hate the darkness during the day?"

"During the daytime, I open the shutters." Mister Blekkink looked away. "I do not have a wife. She died of the pox twelve years ago, the first year we were here."

Twelve years and yet it was obvious the pain remained. "I . . . I can't imagine what it must be like to lose a loved one. Leaving my parents and brothers and sisters behind in Scotland was horrible. But some day I hope to see them again. You must get awfully lonely."

He touched my shoulder causing me to flinch. I thought he was going to squeeze me again.

His pale eyes opened wider, and he smiled. "Oh, I am not alone, laddie. My daughter, Lotte, lives with me. She has fixed a fine supper just for you. You will see."

This stubby strong man was full of surprises.

A moment later, Mr. Blekkink, with my wooden chest perched on his shoulder, and what looked to be a fine musket in his other hand, tapped the front door of the house with the butt of the rifle. "Lotte . . . Lotte, it is your Pa and Mister Hamish."

I stood at the entrance, my burlap bag slung over one shoulder, as several locks were slid and the door opened flooding the small stone porch in light.

I took half-a-step back. I was expecting a little girl not the young woman with long blonde tresses splayed over her shoulders who answered the door.

Chapter Seventeen

I stepped into Hans Blekkink's home, my boot scuffing on the wooden plank floor. Lotte moved in front of me, blocking my path. She looked up at me, her blue eyes scanning my face. Like her father she was short, but thank goodness she wasn't built like him. She was slender with curves where they belonged. Her face was . . . was perfect. A small nose, rosy cheeks kissed by high cheek bones, a round dimpled chin, red puffy lips, and the strangest color of eyes, like a very pale sky, that sparkled with the dancing candle-light. "You can leave your baggage here by the stairs and your coat as well."

I shed my coat, heavy with the pistols. "I . . . I didn't know Mister Blekkink had a daughter. My name is Hamish, Hamish MacCardle." I extended my hand.

Taking my coat, she waved my offered hand away. "You need not introduce yourself to me, and I love your brogue. You are all Pa has talked about since he received your acceptance letter. I feel like I already know you. Thank God you are finally here." She glanced at her father. "Maybe now we can talk about something else."

"No, no, my dear. There is so much more we need to learn about Mister MacCardle."

"There is not much to know," I said. "But I know very little about you and your family."

"Would you like to remove the road dust before we eat?" Lotte asked pointing at a basin and towel on a nearby stand.

"I would," I said rolling up my shirt sleeves.

"When you finish, please come sit at the table, eat, and we will talk, all of us," Lotte said.

Concerned with getting caught staring, I forced my eyes from Lotte. I scanned the interior of the house. The room was spotted with light from ten or fifteen candles and the remnants of a cooking fire in the deep-hearth fireplace that centered the space. Unlike the exterior, the interior walls were wood planking like the floor. The entire first floor was divided into two rooms. To the left of the chimney was a wall with a door in the center. The rest of the large 'L'-shaped area was filled with furniture, two couches, numerous chairs, stools, and a large dining table surrounded by six wooden chairs. Against the left wall near the front door, stairs rose up through the ceiling.

With my hands scrubbed clean, I sat down across from Mister Blekkink as Lotte served pork, potatoes, pork gravy, and fresh green beans, bread, and milk.

"I picked the beans from my garden today and squeezed that milk from Betsey just before you arrived," she said with pride.

"It all looks wonderful," I said with a smile.

"Pa always says grace," Lotte said, nodding at her father and offering me her hand as did he.

Her warm, dainty hand, though, calloused, embraced mine as if I were family.

Holding hands and saying grace brought back fond but greatly missed memories of home.

When we finished eating, I pushed back from the table. "This was a better meal than any I ate in Philadelphia," I said. "Thank you so much, you are a fine cook."

"That she is, laddie," Mister Blekkink added.

"You are both very welcome," Lotte said smiling.

"Tell me, Hamish, what kind of guns were you making when you left Scotland?" Mister Blekkink asked.

Lotte took the question as an opportunity to clean the table.

I stood and helped her, which I had always done at home for my mom. "Ol' man MacDonald made a forty-eight-inch barrel, .50 caliber rifle with a smooth bore. A fine shooting gun, considered accurate up to a hundred yards. What do you make?"

"A smooth bore accurate at one hundred yards?" Mister Blekkink questioned. "Interesting. We will have to talk about how he did that later."

Mister Blekkink also rose and walked to a cabinet and removed three tulip-shaped glasses and a corked clay bottle. He turned to face me. "I make the King's Arm Musket for the British Army which I assume you know all about; a .765 caliber, 46-inch smooth bore barrel. And I make a similar weapon for the locals except it is a .50 caliber. But what I make and what we are going to make are two different things. I want to start making a 48-inch barrel, .40 caliber rifle with a spiraled rifling bore. The theory is if you can make a smaller ball spin through the air it will go faster, farther, and more accurately. My hope is to make a weapon accurate at over two-hundred yards, maybe even three-hundred. Think you can help me?"

"Spiral rifling, sounds interesting, but difficult, but not as difficult as accurate at three hundred yards." I smiled. "Yes, sir, I'd love to help."

"Think of spiraling as a challenge, not difficult." He held up the bottle. "This is my last bottle of *oude jenever,*" he said, stressing the Dutch words. "Jenever is an old Dutch gin that's traditionally drank from these tulip glasses. I've been saving it for a special occasion, and I can think of no better one than this. Will you join Lotte and I in a drink, Hamish?"

"It would be an honor, sir. Though I am not much of a drinker. Every penny I earned went to my family." The last sentence had just slipped out. I wished I hadn't said it. I had been taught family matters were not to be publicized.

"Then one drink of this should be plenty," Lotte said.

He handed out the glasses, filled them to the brim, and raised his in a toast. "To our future successes."

We clicked glasses, and Mister Blekkink and Lotte drank the entire glass so I did as well. I had never tasted anything so harsh or burning in my life. It reminded me of some of my mother's home-made medicines.

"Ahhh, so good; reminds me of home." Mister Blekkink set his glass on the table, and walked to the front door. "I have something to show you." He took a lantern off a wall hook, lighting it with a candle. "Something you may need to know. Come with me." He walked over to the steps by the front door.

I followed him.

He pointed at the door to the left of the hearth. "That is my office and my bedroom. Upstairs is Lotte's room, two other bedrooms, and my store room. Come."

I followed his silhouette up the stairs to a hallway that divided the house front to back. Four doors, two on each side, interrupted the hall.

Lantern held high, he opened the first door in the back of the house. He entered, filling the room in light, and I followed.

"Oh my," escaped my lips involuntarily. Two of the walls were stacked with rifles. In the far corner of the room, farthest from the exposed chimney, were at least a dozen of what I knew to be the standard small kegs of gun powder. Many powder horns topped the kegs. The third wall was lined with shelves of food and what I assumed to be twenty or more jugs of water.

Mister Blekkink picked up one of many bags on top of a table against the fourth wall. "These are marked bags. Each contains different caliber balls, and there are also marked bags of matching caliber wadding." He waved an arm at the stacked weapons. "All ninety of these weapons have been ordered, most by the British Army and almost all paid for; they just haven't been delivered yet." He looked at me and smiled.

"All of the guns are loaded, just not primed," Hans continued. "If we are ever attacked, this house is our fort. So if you hear a bell clanging, that's the signal a watch tower has sighted attackers and everyone is supposed to go to the fort. Do not. Come here. We cannot let either the French or the Indians take this house and all of this. Lotte is as good of a shot as me, and I'm quite good. With our rapid fire power, we should be able to hold off a large force of attackers."

"But, sir"-I shook off my thoughts. I was an indentured servant. It was not my place to challenge this man. He owned me for the next seven years.

"What?" he asked.

"It isn't my place to challenge you, sir."

"What? Speak."

I hesitated.

"Hamish. You and I need an understanding. Yes, you are contracted to work for me for seven years. And I am your boss, yes, but I am not your master. You are not my servant like that piece of paper decrees. You have a debt you must work off, that is all. I respect your opinion, Hamish. Please, always voice your thoughts. I cannot react to silence, nor will I ever get to know you if you do not state what is on your mind. And call me, Hans, Mister Blekkink was my father. Speak, son."

I scratched my head. "With nothing but respect and admiration for your position, sir, since it was just you and Lotte here before, now that I've arrived I can help you move all of these materials to the fort. Don't they have a storage area where they would be safe?"

"Yes, they do. There are several gunsmiths here who have done that."

"Don't you think we'd be safer at the fort with all of the other hundreds of town's people? Also this house has four sides, and there are only three of us."

"Your thinking is sound," Hans said. "But you lack some information. The fort is a long way from here. It is across town tucked in a loop of the Conestoga River, so three sides of it are protected by the river. The river is shallow but wide. So crossing all of that water to attack the fort cannot be done quickly or quietly. I understand why they built it there. It is just that if we are attacked, I do not want to risk taking Lotte all that way. Depending on where the attack comes from, we could be cut off from the fort and caught in the open. Here, we have a chance. And yes, there are four sides and only three of us. But the house is strong and the doors and window shutters are four-inches thick. We will know if anyone is trying to breech an unprotected side long before they do."

"What if they come at night, and I am in the shop?"

"It is also made of stone and houses a small arsenal."

I swallowed hard. "Then, I will be here for you . . . Hans."

Chapter Eighteen

With the exception of Philadelphia, where I slept by myself in a large hotel in the middle of a big city inhabited by many thousands of people, I had never in my life slept in a room alone. On this, my first night in Lancaster Town, I found myself alone in the loft of a gunsmith's shop on the edge of an Indian-infested wilderness. And I was expected to sleep?

I understood why Hans had put me here. I was a stranger in a man's home who had a mature daughter. I would've done the same thing.

Though the shop smelled like sintered iron ore, a smell that ignited thoughts of home and ol' man MacDonald's forge, the loft had been thoughtfully made into a bedroom. There was a small fireplace for heat in the winter months, a large bed, a writing table and chair, extra candles, several windows for ventilation in the warm summer nights like tonight, and a cabinet to store my clothes.

The only thing my new bedroom lacked was being connected to the main house and other people. The stone shop was a good hundred yards from the house; a long run if hostiles were in close pursuit.

I still had Hans's pistols, which I'd return tomorrow. Also, I had at least ten new functional rifles with bullets, wadding, and powder horns which I had lugged up to the loft.

Like the house, all of the first-floor shop windows had their thick shutters closed and barred shut by stout boards slid into iron arms ensconced into the stone walls. The heavy two-door entry, the only walk-in entrance in the building, had the same means of being locked.

But I was still alone, engulfed in blackness.

And there were still who knows how many white-men-hating-Indians lurking in the woods across the clearing.

Every time I laid down and closed my eyes, I saw this image of a copper man with long hair, his face contorted by hatred, with a jagged wide scar from his temple to his jaw. He and many others like him had killed the men in the nearby watchtower before they could ring the bell. Now this group of butchering hostiles were outside the door to the gun shop, chopping and hacking at the wood.

After I was able to mentally eliminate the re-occurring images and get my heart rate back to normal, I relaxed and closed my eyes. I was on the verge of sleep when an owl hooted outside.

Or was that an Indian signaling another savage?

I bolted to my feet. I rushed to the loft's window and peered into the darkness. I couldn't see anything; just blackness, an attacking savage's friend.

But I was safe. All the stone shop's entries were barred shut.

Or were they?

I grabbed the pistols, tucked them into my breeches, clasped a lit candle between my teeth, and climbed down the ladder. Then I checked each window and the double doors to make sure they were all secure.

Then, sweating, I'd climb back to the loft, put the pistols aside, set the candle in a holder, and get back into bed.

Just when I'd get my mind and heart calmed down, another owl would hoot, or a tree branch would bang against a window, and I was up again.

I kept at least two candles burning all night. And I must have climbed up and down the loft ladder a dozen times checking and checking the always barred entrances.

Sleep was not to be had.

I wondered if I would ever be able to sleep alone in this loft.

Chapter Nineteen

A horrendous banging on the shop doors jerked me out of my first brief sleep of the night.

Indians!

My heart pounded in my chest.

Fisting the pistols, I rushed to the loft window above the doors. Though the sun wasn't visible, it was first light.

Hans stood at the doors. My shoulders sagged with relief.

Exhausted from the lack of sleep and taunting fear, I clamored down the ladder and opened the doors in the same clothes I'd arrived in yesterday. Using my forearm, I wiped sweat from my forehead.

"Hamish, *goedemorgen*," he said slipping into Dutch. Then his eyes scanned me. "Are you well? Did you not sleep?"

Hans Blekkink had been so kind and accomodable. I didn't want to complain about anything, especially lack of sleep which was my problem. "I . . . I'm fine. I just fell asleep in my clothes."

"You get changed into some work clothes. Lotte is preparing breakfast. After we eat, you and I will tour the town and come back here. Then we will work on spiral rifling."

"Very good," I said through a yawn.

Hans and I left his barn in his horse-drawn two-passenger carriage and turned onto a country lane.

"I am glad to have this chance to talk to you," Hans said as we rolled past farms. "As I see it, Hamish, you are an investor in my business. You have invested seven years of your life. That is a large investment." He glanced at me.

I nodded, though I had never thought of it in these terms.

"I currently have enough orders, most from the British Army, to keep us working long days for at least two of those years, maybe three."

He negotiated a turn in the lane and the city lay before us.

"But as my biggest investor, there is something I need to share with you. The gun business in the British America has changed due to the progress made with rifled barrels by the local German gunsmiths; primarily those craftsmen here in Lancaster. It is now divided into two markets; rifled weapons versus smooth bore."

Hans pointed at the smooth bore rifle I was carrying. "The British Army still wants smooth bore weapons because of loading issues and fouling problems with the rifled barrels. Their orders are for replacement weapons for those broken, lost, or stolen."

"Slow now, Anke." Hans pulled the reins, slowing the horse. "However, the local people here want rifled barrels for range and accuracy because they depend on hunting for food. Also this war has raised the need for accuracy. It is one thing to have an army of men firing a wall of lead versus being alone in the wilderness trying to protect your family. You need to make every shot count and the farther the better. Gives a single shooter time to reload."

He sighed. "The market in the British America among the locals is growing beyond the needs of the British. If I do not gain a share of the local market, I estimate I will be forced out of business within the next three years by my competition." He took in a deep breath and released it. "If that happens, regrettably, we will both have to work for someone else. I will have no choice; I will have to sell the contract I have with you."

As we entered the city, I tried to imagine what my life would be like without Hans and Lotte. During my journey from Scotland, I had been told countless times how indentured servants were treated as slaves in the New World. Maybe Hans was the exception; different than the other gunsmiths. I pushed the thought aside. I wanted to enjoy what I had.

"We must start making a rifled barrel weapon, like the locals Germans are making; a longer range and more accurate weapon," Hans continued. "But if we can make an even better weapon than my competitors, than our business will thrive."

As we entered a street lined with houses and busy people, we rolled toward the morning sun.

Hans held up a finger. "One, I do not want to lose my business, and," he held up a second finger, "two, I do not want to work for anyone else. I worked hard most of my life to make someone else successful. That is why I came here, to have my own business."

His words brought my nod. I knew all about working hard to make someone else successful.

"But I am going to need help to make such a weapon. I contracted with you because I needed help in meeting my current orders. But now I need both your skills and your dedication." Hans turned onto another street heading south. People were everywhere, walking, riding horses, in carriages.

I wasn't sure I could help him. Ol' man MacDonald and I created some changes that greatly improved the range and accuracy of his smooth bore rifles. But we had not made a weapon like Hans was trying to make, not even close.

"I must do this, Hamish . . . for Lotte. I want to send her home, back to the Amsterdam where she'll be safe, Also, she wants to go to Utrecht University. Women are accepted in universities there but not here. She is very bright and would love to get a higher education in the arts and music. At home, she was considered a gifted cello player. You will see. After she gets to know you, she may play for you. She is shy about her music."

My eyes slid from Hans's intense face to the sidewalk sliding by. His words were like a cannon ball dropping into my stomach. Lotte was both beautiful as well as nice to me. I didn't want Lotte to leave. I wanted to hear her music. I wanted to . . . I refocused, looking at the street. I was pinched. If successful, Lotte would leave, if not, I could be another man's slave for seven years. I shook off my selfish thoughts.

I set my jaw.

Though I barely knew this block of a man, I believed his every word. And if Lotte's dream was to return to the Amsterdam, I'd help Hans make it happen.

"Hamish, you have not said a word. What do you think?"

"You are such a kind and considerate man. I . . . I don't want you or I to work for anyone else." I clapped my hands together. "I can't wait for us to get back to the shop and get started."

He slapped me on the back with one of his strong hands, sliding me almost off the seat.

"Do you think we can make this rifle?" Hans asked, smiling.

I nodded, returning his smile. "Yes. Yes, I think we can." I, for one, wouldn't stop until we did.

We had to have traveled two miles to get to the fort on the southeastern edge of town. No wonder Hans chose not to come to the stockade if an attack occurred.

Tucked into a crook of what Hans had said was the Conestoga River, the fort's walls rose up to twenty feet in places. When we passed through the gates, the walled-interior sprawled before us. The enclosed area had to be close to forty acres, more than enough for all of the town folk to relocate inside during an attack.

As George Hastings had said, the stockade had a large storage area for munitions and food from the several local gunsmiths and surrounding farmers.

Lancaster was ready for a siege.

After a brief tour of the fort, Hans guided the buggy through the streets of town toward his home.

We turned a corner to encounter a crowd of people blocking the street. They were all yelling, many of the woman crying, all on the verge of total disorder.

We could see two men on horses in the distance, in the center of the gathering.

Hans stopped the rig, and we got out and wove our way through the crowd. The closer I got to the mounted men, both the smell and the features of the men slammed me. A few more steps and I could distinguish the charred and bloody British uniform with sergeant's strips on one of the two men and the remnants of red hair on the other.

Alongside of Hans, I broke out of the crowd into a small circle where two men held the reins of skittish horses. Though the horsemen had been scalped, their eyes-gouged out, and burned, I recognized them; the Sergeant of my coach's military escort and the red-headed boy from the group of scalp-hunting young men from Reading. Their corpses were held upright, strapped to wooden braces tied to their saddles.

I bent over as my breakfast erupted from my mouth.

Hans supported me as I emptied my stomach and continued to gag.

I could picture what had happened to the rest of them. May God have mercy on their souls and the souls of all eighteen of them.

I would never sleep again.

"I'll ask one more time, does anyone know these men?" one of the men holding the reins asked the crowd.

Pushing upright, I raised my hand. Hoping I could control myself enough to speak.

Hans and I rode back to his home in silence.

Upon arrival, I helped him unharness the horse. Then we put the horse to pasture and the rig in the barn.

As he hung the traces on a wooden peg, he turned to me. "Hamish, I can not imagine how you must feel having known those men and the boys as well."

Since recognizing them, I could not rid my mind of thoughts about what those men and boys must have gone through. My insides quivered as the vision of their mutilated bodies flashed in my head, again. I closed my eyes hoping to block the vision only to make it sharper, clearer. I prayed they had all been killed quickly, hopefully in the fight, before the mutilation had begun.

I had no response. I busied myself straightening and hanging up the harness with shaking hands.

He shook his head. "I must say no one ever gets use to the lurking horror here. But those of us who have lived in the wilderness for a while, at least we are very aware of its existence. We forget how shocking it is to a newcomer, particularly someone from a large civilized Scottish city, like yourself."

Hans's words restored the vivid images of the Sergeant and boy, bringing a strange and yet horribly associated thought. What the Indians had done to them wasn't that different than what the Reading soldiers had done to the Indians staked outside the fort.

And how uncivilized was it for the group of Reading young men to scalp and most likely kill Indian children for money?

I finished my work and stood there looking out into the clearing, the no-man's land. Based upon everything I'd seen in this white versus red conflict, there was no good side; just evil.

Did evil lurk inside everyone, including me? Driven by anger, I had done an evil deed. May God forgive me, I had killed. But that was different, or was it?

Did it take war to create enough hate to bring this extent of evil out in men? Were all men capable of killing or even worse, torturing someone to death?

If this is how war affected men, I didn't want any part of it. Unfortunately, I had no where else to go. I was trapped.

Hans kicked a block of wood against one of the rig wheels to keep it from rolling. "I had assumed you had a problem-free trip here from Philadelphia, but I was wrong, so wrong."

I nodded.

Hans gently touched my shoulder. "I have changed my mind about what we will do today."

Hans, Lotte, and I spent the rest of the day moving his office and bedroom from the first-floor of his house to one of the second-floor rooms in the back of the house. He said he wanted to sleep back there so he could keep an eye on his out buildings.

Then we moved the furnishings and weapons from the shop's loft to the first-floor bedroom that was previously Hans's room.

After finishing the move, Hans wiped sweat from his brow. "Now maybe you will be able to sleep, Hamish."

Twenty

After a dreamless, restful sleep in my new room, a boom of thunder caused me to stir and get up. I stretched and peeked through a slot in the shutters. It was barely daylight and raining hard.

A pot clanged in the kitchen, just outside my door. Someone was up. I washed the sleep off my face, ran my hands through my sleep-matted hair, and dressed.

I stepped out closing the door behind me. I wanted to freeze this moment in my mind. The first of hopefully many mornings to come in my new home.

Lotte stood bent over in front of the burning fireplace wearing a faded gray, homemade housedress, similar to the ones my mom wore.

My presence startled her upright, and she checked her bun-tucked blonde hair.

"Good morning, Hamish," she said, removing a frying pan with a skirt-wrapped hand. "I hope my banging pots around out here didn't wake you. Pa always told me it never bothered him, but I think he was just being kind." Her pale blue eyes met mine.

For a long second or two, her stare froze me. Despite her commoner's attire and wound hair, she was heart-stopping. "Your father is kind; I love my new room," I said, brushing my hair off my forehead. "And no, you didn't wake me, the thunder did."

"I've boiled some tea if you'd like a cup." She pointed at the black pot hanging inside the hearth. "And I'll have some rabbit fried in a minute, along with these eggs." She raised the skillet in her covered hand. "I tried to buy some parritch just for you, since I know Scottish folk eat that for breakfast. But the old man at the market didn't have any. He said my best bet was to ask Frank, the coach driver, to bring me some. And I will. Frank's a friend." She returned the skillet to the hearth.

"Pa should be down any minute," she said, not waiting for my response. "How did you sleep? After what you and Pa saw yesterday . . . I'm just glad I wasn't with you."

"Amazingly, I slept soundly, thanks to you and your father." I sat down at the table.

A few moments later, Lotte walked over and spooned the sizzling rabbit into a bowl and covered it with a plate. She hesitated standing next to me. She smelled like the fireplace. "I hope what I'm about to say comes out right." She sighed and then touched my shoulder with her free hand.

No one had ever made me tingle before by touching me, not even my mom.

"I must echo my father's feelings for I too am glad you're here," she said. "Pa is getting too old to work as hard as he does. I pray you being here reduces his work day."

"That shouldn't be a problem. I've been trained to work hard. Ol' man MacDonald, my mentor, had me working fourteen-hour days since I was ten-years-old."

"I will not be doing that," Hans's deep accented voice came from behind me at the foot of the stairs.

Lotte's hand slid from my shoulder as we both turned to face her father.

"Good morning, sir," our voices echoed.

"What happened to 'Pa' and 'Hans'?" he asked, shaking his head. Then he chuckled softly as if to himself.

Lotte glanced at me and smiled, the candle light reflecting in her pale eyes.

I couldn't stop my smile.

I was home.

Chapter Twenty- One

After a hearty breakfast of rabbit, eggs and corn dodgers and a rainy run from the house, Hans and I wiped off our wet heads with an old shirt he kept in the shop.

"I am so excited," Hans said as he flung the shirt aside. "Today we will see if we can do spiral rifling." He walked over to a cabinet. "I've made some tooling, but I haven't tried it because it takes two sets of skilled hands. And I am not sure it will work." He reached into the cabinet and removed what looked to be a very small diameter spring that had to be close to five feet in length. He handed it to me.

I held the long drooping spring up to my eyes. "This is hard to gauge only being twisted maybe two times over its entire length. But I'd say it's about a .40 caliber diameter. Correct?" I asked.

Hans smiled. "You have a good eye, Hamish."

"That was easy, you told me you wanted to make a forty caliber barrel." I held the spring by one end, raising my arm straight up and scanned it from one end to the other. "Ol' man MacDonald was always giving me books to read. Books I loved. Books by wise men from centuries past; men like Galileo and DaVinci. DaVinci would have called this a helix."

Hans's eyes enlarged. "Exactly. I doubt if many of the master gunsmiths here would have known the proper name for this shape." He spread his thick arms. "Seems to me, this MacDonald fellow produced more than guns, he also made an educated journeyman."

"I'm not educated. I had to quit school when my father left home to find work in England. I was ten, the oldest of four children. I had to go to work. Fortunately for me, master gunsmith MacDonald hired me to do clean-up work for him. One day he gave me a little project to work on and after that he tested my mental and hand skills with more and more challenging jobs. A year or two later, he started to give me things to read. Books about math and science, simple books at first. And as I progressed so did the books. But believe me, ol' man MacDonald got back every minute he invested plus some. I worked long days for barely enough to keep my family fed for years and years. Thank God my father finally came home." I handed the helix back to Hans. "Enough about me. Why is this helix only twisted maybe twice over what looks to be five feet?"

"A friend of mine served his apprenticeship in Germany," Hans said. "He told me the Germans found that the number of revolutions of barrel grooves affect a ball's spin rate and stability in flight. The larger the ball, the smaller the twist rate; the smaller the ball the higher the twist rate. They determined over years of testing that for a 50 caliber ball, one revolution of twist per 42 inches of barrel length was ideal. For our 40 caliber ball, and a 48-inch barrel, two twists."

"Interesting. Ol' man MacDonald always said the Germans were both smart and dependable because they tested their ideas. Tell me more about this tool, and why you don't think it will work."

"This tool is supposed to be a guide for a cutter tool that fits inside the helix and is hammered through the bore cutting eight spiral grooves at once. Another number the Germans told my friend was good."

"That sounds as if it would work," I said, picturing his words.

"The problem is the cutting tool has to be hammered and the helix had to be made of small stock to fit inside a forty caliber barrel. My fear is that every time the cutter is struck, the helix will move inside the barrel causing the groove to be anything but spiraled."

I took the spring back from him and rolled it in my fingers. "Do you have a forty caliber barrel here that you were going to groove?"

Hans returned to the cabinet and retrieved a barrel.

I took the bored-out piece of iron in one hand and the helix in the other. I tried to slide the end of the helix into the opening. I had to put the barrel on a bench and align the helix to get it started. The fit was tight, too tight, and the helix too pliable. It was like trying to push a rope.

I straightened. "I think I can fix your problem."

"I am listening," Hans said.

"Let's heat the barrel until the bore enlarges. Then we'll insert the helix. Then we'll compress the guide tool, enlarging its diameter until it's tight, very tight. We will then hold the compression while the barrel cools. The resulting friction should restrain the helix no matter how much you hammer on the cutting tool."

"You are a genius. I think that will work." Hans chuckled and patted my shoulder. "Let us try it."

Three hours later and several adjustments, including scrapping the first barrel attempted, Hans and I finished cutting spiral scores into a barrel.

Hans checked the barrel. "Oh my God, we have done it!" he screamed, setting the barrel down and hugging me. "Now all we have to do is make a deeper cut."

"How do we do that?" I asked.

Hans smiled and removed another cutting tool from his cabinet. "This tool has a slightly larger cutter diameter for it's eight blades. We just need to align its cutters with the grooves we made. I thought it would be easier to make two cuts rather than one deep one."

"These tools are the work of a genius," I said, taking my turn to smack his shoulder.

Thirty-minutes later, we had finished our first spiraled rifling. We heated the barrel and removed the helix.

Hans held the barrel up to a lantern and inspected it. "Hamish, it is a thing of beauty. Eight lovely rotating grooves over the entire length." He handed the rifled shaft to me.

I held it up to the light. "Aye." I glanced out the window. "The rain has stopped. Like the Germans, we need to test our creativity. Let's assemble the gun, and take it along with a smooth barrel rifle of the same caliber and compare their accuracy over the same distance."

Chapter Twenty-Two

Hans and I stood in the clearing inspecting the shaved face of an iron ore blackened maple stump. We were about halfway between the barn and the woods, and for safety's sake, close to one of the towers.

"I don't understand it," Hans said with a grimace on his face. "The ball is on line but dropping almost eighteen inches in one-hundred-fifty yards."

"At least it was on line, got this far, and punched a deep hole into the hardwood." I held up the musket I was carrying. "Who knows where the ball went from this unrifled gun. There's no mark on the stump. And both weapons were fired from the same gun stanchion."

Hans looked around and held up a hand. "The air is still. There is no wind. There can be only one reason for that big of drop. We have to get the speed of the ball up to not only make the weapon accurate at this range but to extend the range. I want a gun that shoots within a few inches at two hundred yards if not longer." He sighed and stared at me.

"We could always add more powder," I said.

"According to the British, these barrels with rifling already have a problem with fouling," Hans said. "They *must* be cleaned too often to be useful in combat."

I nodded, acknowledging the fact known within the craft. "Yes, the powder residue gets into the rifled grooves." I glanced away. "Ol' man MacDonald told me the Germans have experiments with spiral-cut barrels going back for at least one-hundred years. He also said their rifled muskets wouldn't shoot further with accuracy until recently. He had figured out how they did it. Although MacDonald never rifled his weapons, he made a smooth-bore rifle that would shoot within four-inches at one hundred yards which was a precedent."

"What did he do?" Hans asked.

"He increased the speed without adding more powder. Let's go back to the shop. There are a couple of things we need to check."

As Hans took a step toward the shop, movement across the clearing caught my eye. An Indian stepped from behind a tree in the woods, taking my breath. I grabbed Hans's arm and gasped some air. "Look." I pointed.

Hans turned, his eyes following my pointed finger, and immediately started to load the rifled musket we'd assembled.

"He's just standing there," I said. "He's not moving. He thinks he too far away to be hit."

Hans finished loading the weapon. "I pray he comes back in a few days when we've improved this gun."

"I pray you're right, at least about improving the gun."

Hans looked at me for a long moment. "Why do you say that in such a way? You would not shoot him if you could?"

I shrugged. "As long as he isn't threatening us, why would I shoot him?"

"Because he is an Indian and that by itself is a threat. Have you forgotten what we saw in town yesterday?"

I closed my eyes and shook my head. "No, I will probably never forget that. But how do you know he's a bad Indian. Maybe he has never hurt a white person. And maybe he and his tribe are friends with the British. One of the men in my coach coming here said many of the local tribes are friendly."

"Thoughts like that will get you killed out here, Hamish. Your first thought should always be no Indian is a good Indian."

Before I could respond, the men in the tower nearest to us, began clanging a bell.

"Should we run to the house and get ready for an attack?" I asked, as calmly as my knotted stomach would allow.

"No," Hans said as he returned a wave from one of the men in the tower. "But load your weapon. We need to stay here so you can see what happens."

Within minutes, thirty-to-forty armed men either on foot or horseback came running to the tower whose bell continued to clang. The men stopped near the tower and talked to the men who had climbed down.

"All of the men in Lancaster are trained to get weapons and rush to any clanging tower in the area where they live. If the bell-ringing tower is not directly near where a man lives, he is supposed to gather his family, weapons, and food and go to the stockade."

"The whole town is heading for the fort at this very minute because of one Indian?" I asked.

"Yes. There could be hundreds right behind the one we saw. We cannot take a chance. This war has come home. Last month, hundreds of French and Indians attacked Fort Augusta just a day's ride north of here. When the attackers found the fort too well defended, they left. We have settled into what they think is their territory. They will not stop until either they defeat us or we them."

Several of the mounted men bravely galloped to where the Indian had been spotted in the woods. They explored the area and returned shaking their heads.

"What will they do now, call everyone back from the fort?" I ask.

"No," Hans said. "This could be a trap. A large force may be watching and waiting for everyone to leave the fort and then attack. The attackers could catch us off guard and be able to get between the townspeople and the stockade. The plan is to post many sentries around the town for the next several days before allowing the townspeople to go back to their homes. The fort's commandant makes the call when they can return to their homes."

The thought of being attacked almost made me ill. I knew I would become another animal like the rest of them to prevent Lotte or Hans from being captured and tortured.

"So you, Lotte, and me are going to stay out here in the house and not go to the fort like everyone else for the next few days?"

"That is correct. Boarded up and ready. But first you and I will go back to the shop so you can show me what ol' man MacDonald had figured out to gain accuracy over distance with a smooth bore musket."

Chapter Twenty-Three

Hans and I returned to the shop as several of the townsmen commenced to set up an encampment between the towers.

"What are those men doing out there?" I asked.

"When there is an alarm, there are groups of men assigned to camp between all of the towers around the town. Their purpose is to slow down an immediate attack to give the locals time to get to the fort. They will stay there either until there is an attack, or until all of the people return to their homes."

"Great plan," I said nodding my head. "Sounds like the Commandant is a smart man."

"Yes, he's good. He attributes his knowledge to what the Indians have taught him. He has scars to remind him. He was one of the few to survive the Braddock campaign last year." He sighed. "Now back to what ol' man MacDonald taught you."

"May I borrow a caliper?" I asked.

"Certainly, what do you want to measure?"

"The diameter of your 40 caliber musket balls as well as the inside diameter of your 40 caliber barrels."

"That is not necessary. I can save you the time. The inside diameter of my 40 caliber barrels are .400

inches and the diameters of my 40 caliber balls are .370 inches. Quite different from the King's Arm Musket with a .765 caliber bore and a .69 caliber ball."

"And like the weapons we shot today, you always use paper wadding, right? You put in a measured amount of gun powder followed by a wadding-wrapped ball tamped down the length of the barrel so the wadding keeps both the ball and powder in place. What size is the wadding?"

"The wadding is paper cut or torn, maybe three-quarters of an inch in diameter and paper thin, maybe .005-.010 inches thick," Hans replied. "It must be paper thin to wrap the ball and be easily tamped."

I nodded. "And do you ever use waxed or tallow covered thick paper cushion wads between the powder and wrapped ball?"

"I have them, but normally don't use them. Am I doing something wrong?" Hans asked, arms extended.

"Nothing different than most," I said. "But what ol' man MacDonald found was that with those tolerances, as the charge proceeds down the barrel, the wadding burns away allowing some of the force to blow by the ball so the ball can bounce within the barrel. So you lose both distance and accuracy. MacDonald improved the fit between the ball and the barrel, by making the ball's diameter within .015 inches of the inside diameter of the barrel."

"What?" Hans asked. "But how—"

I held up my hand. "Then he wrapped the ball in very thin, bees wax coated muslin, and yes the wrapped larger ball is harder to tamp, but the speed is greatly increased as is the accuracy because none of the powder explosion blows by the ball. He also used coated cushion wadding, the same caliber as the barrel, between the powder and wrapped ball which also prevented blow by and helped minimize barrel fouling." I swiveled, looking around the shop. "Where's your ball mold? And do you have any muslin and something to make it slippery?"

Chapter Twenty-Four

The sun was on its downward journey, Hans and I stood in the clearing again. We had warned the sentries we'd be doing some test-firing.

Again, we fired both the rifled and smooth bore weapons, just to see what the new sized ball wrapped in oiled muslin along with cushioned wadding would do for both their accuracies. Unlike before, we moved the dislodged stump target closer, to one hundred yards. We shaved a different side of the stump and added a three-inch circle of tar pitch.

This time the smooth bore rifle's ball struck the stump, low and right of the three-inch circle. Maybe six inches low and a few inches wide of the circle, but it hit the stump.

The rifled barrel ball hit just within the tar pitch circle, low but in line with the center.

I was sure the sentries thought there had to something wrong with us as we hugged, slapped, and danced around like we could hear music.

"Let us move the stump back to one-hundred-fifty-yards," Hans screamed, as he kept jumping as if he had fire ants in his pants. "And I love the sights you've added to the front and rear of the barrel. They really help."

"Thanks. We must clean the barrel first, just for the sake of comparing," I said in the middle of a high-stepping jig.

A cleaned rifled barrel later, Hans and I fired another stanchioned-gun round at one-hundred-fifty yards.

We both ran the entire way to the stump; I as fast as I could. I was surprised at how quickly the short man could move. I barely beat him, and I had no problem winning foot races in Scotland.

Panting, Hans dropped to his knees and inspected the stump. "Oh no." Hans shook his head and his shoulders slumped as if his life was being pulled out of him. "We missed." His words fading away.

"That can't be," I said, shaking my head. "Everything is the same. No wind. Same set up of the gun. Same loads. We had to have hit the stump . . . somewhere."

Hans stood and stepped back. "Look for yourself, the same ball holes as before." Hans's head dropped into his hands.

I squatted in front of the stump eyeing the shaved face and running my fingers over the surface. "That's odd," I said.

"What is odd?" Hans raised his shaking head.

I reached behind me and pulled my *sgian-dubh*, my Scottish knife that my dad had given me when he left for England. The knife was a conflicting reminder of my dad's love and his abandonment.

I probed with the tip of the knife into the stump face. A few minutes later, I started laughing and rocking on my knees.

"What?" Hans asked.

I turned to face Hans and held out my hand with two smashed balls in it. "Our second shot at one-hundred-fifty yards hit right next to our first shot from one-hundred yards!"

Hans's shaking head stopped. His eyes enlarged. "Oh my God." Hans grabbed me. "The gun didn't lose any of its accuracy over an additional fifty yards.

Hans leaped in the air. "Oh my, we must try again at two-hundred."

"And two-fifty," I said, standing and hugging him.

Chapter Twenty-Five

By the time Hans and I cleaned the rifle, the light had faded. No more shooting today. We headed for the house and Lotte.

"Well, how did it go out there?" she asked. "I heard the bell clanging and saw all the men arrive. Was that because of your shooting? Were Indians spotted? What's going on? Are we going to be attacked? I was just getting ready to come out there and find out what was going on before I went crazy."

"Sorry," I said. "One of us should've came in and told you. Your dad and I saw an Indian on the other side of the clearing just about the same time a man in the tower did. He sounded the alarm though I didn't think it necessary. Several of the men rode over to where the Indian had been standing and found nothing."

Lotte turned to her father. "So we have to stay buttoned up for a few days, huh, Pa?"

A knock on the front door kept Hans from answering her. He went to the door and peered through a slit. Then he opened it.

A man in a British uniform stood in the entrance.

"Mister Blekkink, we know you and your family stay here during an alarm. I wanted to inform you that the Commandant has decided to release everyone back to their homes before sundown in groups by section of the town. Since this area is the farthest from the fort, don't be alarmed if you see or hear people moving close to dark."

"Thank you, Corporal," Hans said, closing the door and sliding a thick plank into the locking hooks on each side of the door.

"Strange." Hans rubbed his chin. "But probably smart." Then he rushed to Lotte and swooped her up into his arms, causing her to squeak.

"Hamish is such a wise lad, Lotte. He has provided me with the knowledge to make my dream gun." He eased her to the floor. Then he darted at me, engulfed me in his mighty arms, and swung me around like I was a small child.

He put me down and laughed.

I couldn't help but laugh with him, and Lotte joined in.

"We must celebrate!" Hans strolled to his cabinet and took out the tulip glasses and the clay bottle of gin.

I held up my hands. "That is your last bottle, is it not?"

Hans glanced at the bottle. "Yes, why?"

"Then I suggest you save it for when we are consistently accurate over two-hundred yards; hopefully two-hundred-fifty. Maybe tomorrow."

Hans's smile faded and then returned. "You *are* a wise man, Hamish." He returned the glasses and bottle to the cabinet. "I thank God for bringing you to me."

"Tomorrow, Hans. Let's save any praise until tomorrow. Two-hundred yards is a long way. Also, we have some other issues to address."

Hans pulled his head back and squinted as if my words had slapped him. "What issues?"

"A long gun that shoots accurately over two hundred yards is a wonderful weapon but not if it must be cleaned every two or three shots to prevent fouling."

Hans nodded. "Tomorrow."

Lotte held me in her gaze and smiled.

A soft thud awakened me. I sat up and could see nothing but blackness. I shook my head and laid down again. The soft thud returned bringing me to my feet. It was the window shutter hitting the board braced to keep the shutter closed. Someone outside was trying to get inside.

I fumbled in the dark, stubbing a toe. I had to choke down a scream. Finally, I found the pistols. With both weapons cocked and fisted, I eased my way to the window as the thud repeated.

There was somebody out there; I could sense them.

Though my eyes were adjusting to the dark, my nerves weren't. My mouth was dry and my breathing raced with my heart beat.

The British corporal had told Hans that the townspeople would be returning home in groups close to dark based upon the section of town where they lived.

I had no clue what time it was; but I had been sleeping sound. I would guess it to be past midnight.

Why would townspeople be coming home from the fort this late or be behind Hans's house? And why would anybody from Lancaster be trying to get into Hans's house at this hour? By Hans's own words, everyone knew him and had to know he had weapons and could use them.

My logic convinced me only an Indian would be outside the window. My fingers tightened on the wooden pistol grips.

I positioned myself next to the window. The shutters when closed had a small viewing slit between them.

I had to take a chance and take a look. As I took a step to move in front of the window, my foot kicked the chest Hans had sent to me. I forgot that I'd left it in front of the window.

Immediately a knife was jammed though the slit, making me jump.

Driven by fear and anger, I jammed a pistol barrel into the slit and fired.

A man screamed close by the window.

Feet pounded the ceiling above me.

A vision of what these things outside would do to Lotte and Hans if they got inside jolted me.

Still blinded by the flash, I fumbled the other pistol into the slit and fired again.

The shutters banged open in Hans's room above me.

Another shot boomed, followed by another. Lotte had to be up as well.

They couldn't get in.

I moved to an interior wall and found the musket Hans kept on horizontal pegs, primed and loaded. I cocked it, wedged the barrel into the slot, and fired again.

Whether I hit anything didn't matter. I just wanted anyone outside to realize how many guns were in this house. To know they had awakened an arsenal.

Another gun blasted from above.

"Over there!" Hans shouted, followed by another shot.

Then silence.

Long minutes later, gunshots erupted behind the house in the clearing. Some nearby, some not. The sentries. More and more shots followed. There were Indians out there.

My room smelled like burnt gun powder, a smell I knew so well, though it repulsed me tonight.

My knees buckled, dropping my shaking limbs onto the bed.

There would be no more sleep tonight.

Chapter Twenty-Six

I moved to the second floor for the night. My job was to alternate with Hans to watch the back of the house through the remaining darkness. Lotte's room was in the front of the house, and she had gone back to bed to try to sleep. We figured one of us would hear anyone trying to get in the front.

At first light, I leaned out the window and gasped. There were bodies in the yard between the house and shop. Taking my two re-loaded pistols, I ran down the steps.

"Hamish, what is wrong?" Hans asked. "Hamish?" Obviously, he must have glanced out the window. "Oh my God." He thundered down the steps behind me.

I bolted through the kitchen and out the back door. I slid to a stop. Gun-held hands falling to my sides.

The sight and coppery smell of several bodies lying in the grass just behind the house froze me; two Indians and one townsperson; a woman.

Hans rushed out the door, stopping next to me.

"Oh no, did we do this?" I asked, my voice shaking. "Did we kill that poor woman in the darkness?"

"I doubt that," a strange voice said.

I whirled, raising my weapons. A soldier stood at the corner of the house, jerked his hands in the air. "Don't shoot!"

I lowered the pistols.

"Last night, someone, I assume these Indians, tried to break into our house, and the three of us," Hans glanced around for Lotte who hadn't followed, "my daughter as well, started shooting at anything that moved."

"Last night many Indians crawled past our sentries in the clearing," the soldier said. "I guess they thought no one would expect them with the sentries posted. Unfortunately, they broke into several houses and killed quite a few townspeople in their beds. Some of our people tried to run, but were caught in the open which is probably what happened with this woman." He pointed at the body in the grass. "If you check, I doubt if you find any bullet wounds on her body. Thank God, you caught these Indians before they got into your home. Also, your shooting probably saved many other townspeople by waking them. And you alerted the sentries of the attack. Your firing caused the savages to run. Our guards killed many Indians trying to sneak past them."

I couldn't just stand there any longer with an internal argument raging. I had to know. I ran to the woman's body and knelt next to her. She was laying on her stomach, face down. There were no wounds on her back. I would have to turn her over. I hesitated. I had never touched a dead person before. Just thinking about it, made my stomach churn.

Hans must have sensed my plight. He knelt next to me and gently rolled the lady over. The woman had a gash in her forehead, probably from a tomahawk. "I know this woman," Hans said, bowing his head.

A long moment later, rising and helping me to my feet, Hans guided me back to the soldier. "How many townspeople were killed?"

"I'm not sure, maybe twenty or thirty, including a couple of sentries, too many," the soldier said, looking away. His eyes returned to Hans. "Your gun shots saved many."

"How many Indians were killed?" I asked, gazing at the man's body laying just outside my bedroom window.

"I don't know. Not enough."

"No!" Lotte screamed from behind us. "Is that Mrs. Schuman? Oh it is." Her words sagging.

Hans rushed to her and hugged her back into the house.

Back in the house, with Lotte back in her room resting, Hans and I drank strong tea at the kitchen table.

"These Indians are a cunning enemy." Hans said, nodding his head. "This was all planned. They know how we will react to their threats. They had an Indian expose himself yesterday to set off our alarm. Then they hid a few warriors in the grass across the river from the fort. They watched all the residents go into the fort. They continued to watch until we started evacuating yesterday. Then, just as the soldier said, they crawled past our guards and begin breaking into people's homes in the middle of the night. With the sentries posted, they knew we wouldn't expect an attack. They outsmarted us. Thank God you woke up and shot that bastard before he got in."

"You think I shot him?" I said, sitting more upright and shaking my head.

"He was lying right outside your window." Hans said.

I shoved my tea aside, got up, and walked to the front door and went outside. I needed fresh air, and time by myself, time to digest the fact that I had killed again.

Chapter Twenty-Seven

The early morning sun sparkled on the dew covered grass in front of Hans's home.

"Hamish," Hans called, having followed me outside. "Hamish, you are a gun maker. You make an instrument of death. As long as you have been in this business, I would have thought you would have accepted that by now. Guns kill and if you shoot one at someone you may become a killer. It happens everyday in this world."

There had to be a hole in my stomach, leaking acid throughout my gut.

I wished he hadn't followed me. I wanted to be alone. I didn't want to hear his words.

Yes, I had shot through the shutters. I was scared, scared of the hate that was trying to get inside. And yes, at that moment, I had wanted to kill the hate. But to take a life wasn't mine to do. It was wrong. So final.

Hans touched my shoulder. "I know killing changes a man. I know. You lose a piece of your soul; a piece of your humanity. You take a step closer to being a vicious animal. Eventually, I think men either like killing. grow numb to it, or continue to detest it. Either way, they become killers. It's the men whose hate overwhelms their fear that you must be aware of; they are the dangerous ones. And they are not always obvious by their manner. Men I do not care to know; they kill for pleasure." He squeezed my shoulder with his strong fingers. "It does my heart good to see your distaste for killing. We have much in common."

I stared at Hans, chewing on my lower lip. I so wanted to tell him who I was and why I was here. But I couldn't make myself resurrect the ugliness.

I shrugged out of Hans's grasp and walked away, through the grass and down the soldier-strewn lane toward town.

There were a couple of harsh facts I had to face. I had no where else to go. And this war wasn't about to end tomorrow. To survive or to protect my new family, I'd have to kill again and again. Would I then become a soul-less man; a man neither Hans nor I would care to know?

Chapter Twenty-Eight

A day to clean up the town followed by several days of wakes and funerals consumed Hans's, Lotte's, and my time. Though I didn't know the thirty-two murdered people, Hans and Lotte did. They took me wherever they went. Therefore, most of my week was dominated by death, a grim reminder of the reality of life.

Death had slithered into our lives, taking the smiles, the laughter, the joy. Death governed our conversations. It caste the winter's bluntness on our spring. If the birds were singing during the funerals, we never heard them.

I arose at the week's end to the clanging of pans in the kitchen.

I dressed hurriedly and ran fingers through my hair.

I stepped out of my room.

"Good morning, Hamish," Lotte said, standing in front of the fireplace stirring something in a pan suspended over the fire.

I wasn't sure if the fire caused her eyes to sparkle more and her cheeks to have more color, or if there was a change to her demeanor.

"May it be a good morning, Lotte. What is the plan for the day?"

She stepped back from the hearth and placed her hands on her hips. "To let the dead rest and the living live," she said.

"That is a great plan," I said, walking toward the table where I saw a tea kettle steaming.

As I walked past her she grabbed my arm, stopping and turning me to face her.

"I've never thanked you," she said.

"For what?" I asked looking down into her upturned eyes.

She glanced away. "For saving Pa and me the other night." Her pale eyes returned to mine. "Had you not awoke and did what you did, those Indians would surely have gotten into the house."

"But—"

Her warm fingers blocked my words, touching my lips.

Before I could react, she wrapped her arms around my waist and hugged me. I hadn't been hugged since my mother hugged me on the dock in Scotland. But this was different, Lotte's hug seemed warmer, more intense and . . . and a place I didn't want to leave.

I stood there for a second unmoving. Then. as if her warmth had unfrozen me, I wrapped my arms around her and rested my cheek on top of her head.

She squeezed me tighter, causing me to both hear and feel each of my increasing heart beats.

Then she pulled her head back, our faces inches apart.

I was in a place I had never been before, a place making me both feel and think things I had never experienced before. I was no longer in control, something else was. As if someone else was doing it, I leaned down and kissed her. I had never kissed a girl before, never.

My lips lightly on her warm, wet, lips. Her arms left my waist and wrapped around my neck, her hands pulling my head down, pressing our lips together.

All the goodness in this world was here, in her hug, on her lips, with her manipulating hands.

Then a little voice in my head screamed, "This is Lotte, Hans's daughter! She has a dream to go home and pursue a higher education. This is wrong." I pulled back, both breaking the kiss and the hug.

I struggled for both a breath and control. "Lotte, I can't—"

Feet thudded on the steps.

We pushed apart, both gasping.

I hastened to the table and sat, as Lotte straightened her dress and began stirring again.

I couldn't take my eyes off her nor could she stop looking at me, a yearning, wanton look I knew I'd remember for the rest of my life.

Chapter Twenty-Nine
Four weeks later
Summer of 1756

"Hamish, the last musket for the current order of one hundred British Brown Besses is crated," Hans said, his Dutch accent slathered with pride. He patted my shoulder, then closed up the shop. "Thanks to you we are on schedule for delivery. I will leave tomorrow as planned after we pack the wagon."

The sun was a sliver on the western horizon. The past few weeks were a blur. We had talked about this day, and how Hans would take the muskets to Reading and have me stay with Lotte. Now the time had come. I didn't want him to leave. I was afraid of the temptations of being here alone with Lotte. But I didn't know what to say. I had to think of something. "Working with you the time passes so quickly. We have accomplished a lot. I just wish we could have made more of our new rifles."

"The word is circulating that we have made a musket that is accurate within inches at two-hundred-fifty yards. I have been getting a great many queries about our new dream gun from the locals. They are all asking for a demonstration. I plan on giving them one as soon as I get back, God willing. After we show the locals what our weapons can do, I think there will be a bidding war over the ten rifled guns we've made. Can you prepare the shooting range for me?"

I nodded. "I'll clean all of the new rifles we have and set up some targets." We walked a few more steps toward the house. "Are you sure you don't want me to go with you tomorrow? It's a dangerous trip."

"Yes, I am sure. As usual, I will have a military escort. I want you here to protect Lotte in case there is another attack. In the past, she stayed with neighbors when I made deliveries, but that was before things got so bad. If something were to happen, I trust you more than the neighbors."

I had no response. The man was relying on me to watch over his daughter.

"Also, in the five or six days it will take me, you can make another rifled barrel and stock," Hans continued. "I think we will be receiving many orders. That reminds me, as part of our demonstration, we need to show them how easy our new rifle is to load and how many times we can fire it before it requires cleaning. Maybe you could also make a couple of those cleaning rods we created."

"Of course."

Hans slowed his pace. He raised his chin, stretching his short frame to its maximum height. His blue eyes sparkled with pride. "We have done it, Hamish. No one has a weapon with the accuracy over that distance or a quicker way to clean a rifled barrel than we do."

His words gave me a thought. "I could go to Reading in your place. With your connections here, you would probably sell thirty or forty of our new guns in the time that I was gone."

Hans stopped in his walk to the house, halting me by touching my arm. "You must know by now how much I love Lotte. She is my world. And you must realize that I completely trust you to take care of and protect my daughter." He squeezed my arm and then released it. "But something is troubling me. Why don't you want to stay here, Hamish? Is there a problem between you and Lotte? You two barely speak to each other anymore. Did something happen?"

I wondered if Hans could see the lump that had formed in my throat. I held his inquisitive stare, though he was right. Lotte and I barely talked since the kiss.

I glanced away. I couldn't tell him what had happened, and yet I couldn't lie to him. Hans treated me like family, and I loved him for that. He was leaving his daughter's care in my hands, so how could I tell him that I had feelings for her? Nothing had come of the kiss. There was nothing to say about it, except it was a mistake. I had no choice. No matter what, I would honor his trust.

"Lotte and I are fine. You and I have been spending some long hours in the shop, don't think that's a complaint, they were necessary hours to meet *our* commitments." I again fixed on his eyes. "And, unlike working for ol' man MacDonald, I actually have enjoyed the work. Since Lotte isn't interested in what we do, we haven't really anything to talk about and not much time if we did have a subject. I just thought it would be best for our business if you stayed."

Hans started walking again. "You are a smart man, Hamish. What you say makes sense. But it took me a long time to win the trust of Lieutenant Colonel Conrad Weiser. He is different. He doesn't know you, and I doubt if he would give you any more business despite the fact that you work for me. And I want to keep his business. Who knows, maybe I can talk the British into buying some of our new guns" He nodded as he knocked on the back door. "I need to go. Do not worry. Trust me. We will sell more of our new guns than we can make after the demonstration."

Thirty

The sun's glow on the horizon announced its arrival. Lotte and I stood by the loaded Conestoga wagon and looked up at Hans.

"Pa, are you sure you will be safe taking that many guns all the way to Reading. If somehow the French and Indians knew what you were delivering, those eight soldiers going with you from the fort would be of no use. Can't you get more to escort you?"

"We all know the French have spies in Lancaster. The larger my escort, the more interest I arouse. We have done this many times in the past, sweetheart. I'll be fine."

"Yes, Pa, but in the past, the war hadn't come to this area of British America. Now it is here."

"You just worry about making sure Hamish does a full day's work every day while I am gone." Hans looked at me and winked. Then he slapped the reins on the horses' backs and whistled. And the wagon rolled away into the middle of the waiting eight soldiers on the road.

Lotte shook her head and wiped away a tear. "May God look over him."

"I'm sure he'll be fine," I said in with a forced tone meant to persuade myself more than her.

"How can you be sure, Hamish?"

"I can't, Lotte. But your father and I tried to make it as safe as possible. The sides of that wagon are four inches thick and they are high. And I made sure each and every one of those muskets were primed and loaded. If they are attacked, those eight soldiers along with your father can climb into that fort-like wagon and have at least a hundred rounds to fire before reloading. I would like to think you'd be worried about anyone who attacked them."

She blew out a long breath and grinned. "Like Pa always says, you are a good man, Hamish."

I gave her a long look, and wondered if Hans would think I was a good man if he knew all the ways I had imagined kissing his daughter. "You get into the house and board up the doors and windows. And I'll go to the shop. I've got a couple of rifles to make before your Pa gets back."

For the first time, since that crazy moment when we kissed, she looked into my eyes. "I will make you my famous wild boar dinner tonight with all the trimmings. So go work up an appetite." She smiled.

Lotte and I stood frozen in each other's gaze for a moment until a spell-breaking thought came to mind. Hans and I were on the verge of being successful. Which meant he would soon have enough money to send Lotte back to the Amsterdam to college.

I turned and trudged to the shop.

Chapter Thirty - One

The shop wasn't the same without Hans. He was always talking about something; the war, the French, the British, life in the Amsterdam versus British America. His recall of minute details held my interest. Listening to him made me respect his knowledge. I had witnessed his dedication to details every day in his work.

I replaced the silence with the sounds of a billows-fired hot forge and a hammer pounding metal.

Hans ordered the trigger assemblies and flint-locks from other gunsmiths in Lancaster who specialized in only making those parts.

I estimated it would take me three to four days to make a rifled barrel, a day or two to make the stock, and a day to assemble and test fire the weapon. Hopefully, I would have another rifle made by the time Hans got back.

After a long, hot day of operating the forge forming a rough barrel, I was dirty and sweaty. Hans kept a change of clothes and a wash basin in the shop to keep from soiling the house. So as the sun slid beyond the horizon, I washed up and changed clothes before closing up the shop.

After banging my knuckles four hard knocks on the back door, my special knock for Lotte, I heard the board scraping as it was removed from the braces. When Lotte swung the door open, at first I wasn't sure I had the right place. She had on a fresh dress, and had her hair down. As she stepped aside for me to enter, her pale eyes sparkled in the candle light. I had to remind myself to breathe.

As I stepped past her, she closed and boarded the door. I stopped. "We need to talk."

She walked by me. "You can talk while you eat. The food is ready."

We sat at the food-laden table across from each other.

I mapped her features dropping from her captivating eyes sliding down her smooth jawline to her delicate chin and then up to her pink lips. Seconds had to have passed.

"Eat." She broke my stare.

I took a bite of a pork rib and a moan escaped between chews.

"Do you like the wild boar?"

"Delicious," I said and swallowed.

"I'm glad." She pushed the serving plate stacked with ribs closer to me. "We need meat. There is some in the smokehouse, but it's not completely dried yet. Either we go to the town market tomorrow, or we can go hunting. I'm a pretty fair shot."

"Do you think it's safe?"

"Pa and I do it all the time as do most of the townspeople. The area is full of game."

"Then we'll go hunting. You can try our new gun."

"Great. Tomorrow then. Now what do we need to talk about?"

Suddenly my throat was dry. I sat the rib bone down and licked my fingers. I shifted forward and took a drink of water. My eyes diverted from her to watch my fingers slid around the rim of the pewter cup. "When I was a young apprentice, I was taught to never start something I couldn't finish."

She waited for me to continue and when I didn't she canted her head. "And?"

"And your father told me if we were successful in increasing our gun business, he planned to send you back to the Amsterdam so you could go to the university."

She nodded. "Yes. Pa and I had discussed that when he sent for you."

"Well, your Pa and I are close to being successful. We have made a great rifle and people are talking about it. So I think your dream will soon come true."

"And?"

"I should have never kissed you." I looked away, shaking my head.

"Oh." She looked down. "I . . . I liked it."

"Don't misunderstand me, I loved it." The words spilled from my lips before I could think.

Then her eyes sought mine.

I tried to swallow the lump in my throat. "It's just so hard for me to imagine you leaving," I admitted. "And . . . well after our lips touched it," I looked away and cleared my throat, "it made it more difficult to think about."

"I'm glad you don't want me to leave."

"But you should go. You have a chance to pursue your dreams. Few people ever have that chance. Do it. Besides, this place is too dangerous."

"You really loved our kiss? What's a kiss to a good-looking man like you? You've had to have kissed hundreds of girls back in Scotland."

I shook my head. "Never. Never before. Not one. You . . . you were my first."

"Truly?"

My eyes found hers and searched them for her thoughts. Was kissing a normal practice here? Had her lips touched another man's lips? A warm surge not unlike anger flowed through me. But this feeling was worse than anger, I was humbled. She said she liked our kiss, but had she liked others as well?

"You've been kissed before?" I asked, thinking how immature I must seem to her.

"Yes, but only once. Despite Pa's tight reins. I kissed a boy at a dance several years ago. It was just a peck on the lips. It," she shook her head, "it was nothing."

I gazed at her pink lips, remembering how soft they were. I pushed the thought aside. "I wouldn't think your father would be happy to know his indentured servant, the man he left to watch over his only child, had kissed her."

She shrugged. "That may well be, but he likes you a lot."

"And I him." Guilt clung to each word for all I could think about was kissing her. "You need to go back to the Amsterdam."

"Does that mean you're never going to kiss me again?"

I sighed. "Yes."

She pursed her lips. "Never is a long time."

I wanted to jump up and take her in my arms and kiss her and kiss her. But I couldn't. I picked up my boar rib and took a bite. I chewed as if chewing on my own words. I'd be one of those people who never had a chance to pursue his dreams.

Chapter Thirty-Two

The morning light found Lotte and me in the dew-covered clearing between the town and the woods with two of the new rifled muskets. She walked like an experienced hunter, quietly, cautiously, and with a purpose.

"Good morning, Lotte, all is clear this day," one of the men in the tower called to her.

She responded with a wave.

He knew her name. As she said, she must have done this many times in the past with her father.

I followed her.

I had hunted small game in Scotland since I was old enough to shoot. And before that my father had taught me how to trap. But Scotland didn't have Indians and dangerous animals. My senses were peaked. But Lotte's comfort level eased my grip on the gun.

Halfway through the clearing, it was obvious that this area had been hunted out; not even a bird flew over.

Lotte kept going, nearing the treeline.

"Lotte, we're getting too close to the woods and too far from the towers," I whispered.

"If we want to eat, we have to go where the game is," she murmured over her shoulder.

My grip tightened.

When we were within a hundred yards of the dense trees, she suddenly stopped, cocked the musket's hammer, and shouldered her weapon.

I looked past her and saw nothing. And then as if drawn to us, a large doe walked out of the woods.

I moved from behind her and also cocked and raised my gun. As I took my last step to be next to her, I stepped on a branch and snapped it.

To my dismay, the doe bolted just as she shot. The deer fell, apparently hit, and then rose and limped into the trees.

Lotte turned, her cheeks flushed, and grabbed my musket and thrust hers into my hands. Then she sprinted after the wounded animal.

"No!" I yelled and took off after her. I thought of reloading her gun, but she would disappear into the woods before I could.

I entered the forest feeling vulnerable with an empty gun.

I caught glimpses of Lotte plunging through the thick trees in front of me. My inability to protect myself was replaced with my concern for her safety. I pushed my legs to run as fast as I could, dodging trees and ducking branches.

I was gaining on her, just ten or fifteen steps away when she disappeared behind a thicket.

"Ahhhhh!" Lotte's shrill scream made me run faster than I thought I could.

I leaped a log and there she was writhing on the ground.

Heart racing, I slid to a stop next to her.

She bent over, moaning and clutching at her lower leg.

I followed her hands to a pair of metal jaws clamped on her leg just above her boot-covered ankle. Blood flowed between her fingers.

"Oh, Lotte." My stomach heaved as I dropped my gun and knelt by her foot.

Lotte arched her head back and gritted her teeth. Dirt was smeared across her cheek. Her skin growing paler from the pain.

The trap was attached to a chain embedded in the earth. My hands covered hers. "Let go, Lotte."

She released her grip.

I grabbed the jaws and tugged with all my strength moving the jagged teeth slightly and then slipping from the blood, making her scream again. The last thing I wanted to do.

The gunshot, her screams, we had to get out of these woods.

I needed a pry bar. I reached for my gun.

"No!" Lotte cried out. Her body stiffened, pulling my eyes from searching the high grass for my rifle to her face. Her eyes were enlarged, looking behind me.

I swiveled my head around to see a painted-face Indian standing behind me aiming a musket at us. I tried to gulp air but couldn't.

When the Indian saw my face he pulled his cheek off the stock of the gun and stared at me. His black eyes squinted.

My peaked fear bloomed into a shudder when I saw the wide scar on the side of his face. This couldn't be the same Indian I'd seen on my way to Lancaster. The man full of hate.

Lotte was trapped and all I had was an empty gun somewhere nearby.

Was I destined to be killed by this man?

He'd have to kill me because I wasn't going to allow him to touch Lotte.

As if something snapped inside me, my fear was gone, I was calm and in control. I knew what I had to do.

I slowly raised my hands, moving my body enough to shield Lotte.

The Indian motioned me to the side with his gun.

Looking into his black eyes, I set my jaw and slowly shook my head. Somehow, I needed to get to my knife wedged in my waistline in the middle of my back before he killed me.

The red man took a quick step and slammed the gun butt into my shoulder knocking me onto my back.

Though my shoulder burned with pain, I purposely fell onto my arm, allowing my fingers to find the handle of my knife.

The Indian stepped on my chest pinning me as well as my arm. I squirmed and grabbed his leg with my free hand and tried to pull it off me. He again raised the gun butt as if to strike me, and I stopped moving, releasing his leg.

The man had a strange expression on his copper-skinned, red and white striped face. More of a look of frustration than hate.

He removed his foot from my chest and again motioned me away.

Clenching the knife behind me, I pushed a few feet away.

Without taking his eyes off me, he eased the hammer of his gun into the half-cocked position, disarming it. Then he slid the end of the barrel between the jaws of the trap next to Lotte's foot. He put his cloth covered-foot against one of the jaws.

Lotte's face scrunched in pain, she cried out.

The Indian glanced at her, then again fixed his eyes on me. Using the gun as a lever, he forced the jaws apart. Then he grunted at me.

He was freeing her!

This was my chance to stab him, he was defenseless. But this man could have killed me and didn't. Why would he unspring the jaws holding Lotte if he wanted to hurt us?

Getting Lotte out of that trap was her only chance no matter what his intentions.

I slid my knife back into my belt and scrambled to my knees and scurried to Lotte. Though she moaned when I grabbed her calf, I eased her foot out of the trap.

The Indian jerked the rifle barrel free, allowing the jaws to snap closed. Then he stepped away.

I eased Lotte's foot to the ground. She sighed and laid back, her body trembling. She squeezed my arm.

My hand found the handle of my knife, and I turned, jumping to my feet with my knife hand extended.

The man was gone.

Not a branch moved, no sounds; just gone.

I glanced down at the knife in my white-knuckled fist. Unlike him, I'd been driven by fear. This was foolish. Had the man wanted to kill me, I'd be dead. I dropped my knife-holding hand to my side.

"I'm sorry, Hamish." Lotte's voice was reedy as she tried to speak through the pain. "But the animal was wounded and . . . well Pa and I have hunted these woods many times and there were never any traps or Indians."

"Shh, Lotte. I understand. Hold still, I have to stop the bleeding." I put the knife to better use. I cut off the sleeve of my shirt and knelt. I sliced away her torn boot, and carefully cinched my shirtsleeve around her bleeding ankle. "Can you sit up?"

Lotte struggled upright. Her dirt-smudged cheeks scored with tear tracks. Deep tremors shook her body.

We must get out of these woods. Shelving my desire to hold Lotte and comfort her, I retrieved the guns and gave them to her. Then I swooped her up. She was light and warm against me.

She wrapped one of her arms around my neck.

Neither of us said anything.

I carried her out of the woods into the clearing.

Being in the open, in sight of the towers and her home, Lotte's shaking faded. She nestled her cheek into the crook of my neck.

I could feel her warm breath against my neck. Her body against mine. My pounding heart was no longer booming in my ears because of fear, but because of my desire for her.

This was not a good time for Hans to be gone.

"Is Lotte hurt?" a man in the tower yelled. "Do you need help? What happened?"

I started to respond and stopped. The Indian had helped us. I didn't want the townspeople hunting for him. "We're fine. She just hurt her ankle chasing the deer she wounded. I'll take care of her."

And I would.

Chapter Thirty-Three

Lotte stared straight ahead, saying nothing throughout our bouncing buggy trip to the local doctor. An hour later, we headed home with her ankle packed with honey and garlic and freshly wrapped in muslin.

Halfway to the house, I could no longer stand the quiet. "Is the pain horrible?"

"No," she said without looking at me.

I needed to get her to open up, to talk. "It's good that the doctor didn't think you broke any bones. He was very concerned about you walking for a few days, for fear you'd re-open the wounds. But don't worry, I'll carry you wherever you want to go."

Lotte looked at me. Her enlarged eyes filled with dismay. "I cannot believe what happened. I keep going over and over it. It's hard for me to grasp that an Indian with such a scary face wanted to help white people, especially in these times. He could have killed us both. All he had to do was shoot you. I was caught in the trap helpless. He could have done whatever he—"she closed her eyes and shivered.

I gently touched her arm. "Thank God he's a good person," I said, rubbing away her quaking. "It's over. We're safe." I maneuvered the horse so the buggy's wheel missed a deep hole. I glanced at her, her pale blue, red-streaked eyes meeting mine. "I've seen that man before, on the way here from Philadelphia. He probably could have killed me then as well, but didn't." I shook my head. "A man with the ability to block out the hate surrounding him. How can he do that with all the cruel violence happening all around him?"

She grazed my cheek with the backs of her fingers. "He's like you, Hamish, a kind soul." Without caring if anyone saw us, she leaned over, interlocked her arm in mine, and rested her head on my shoulder.

"How are you?" I asked, leaning my head against hers.

"It hurts," she said as she squirmed closer to me. "But the nearer I am to you, the less it throbs."

She made me feel taller, stronger, and so alive. At that moment, I didn't care if someone saw us and told Hans. It didn't matter; nothing mattered but her being snuggled against me.

I pulled the rig up to the front door, hopped out, and carried her into the house. I sat her on a chair. "I'll be right back after I put the horse and carriage in the barn."

I guided the horse-drawn buggy into the barn.

The brush with death had pulled Lotte and me together, closer than the prior lip-peck had. My cheek still tingled from her touch.

Separating the horse from the buggy, I put the gentle animal in her stall. When I stowed the rig and harness, I thought of Hans.

He trusted me.

No one had ever treated me the way Hans had.

The tingling faded.

I trudged to the house. The tension in my body lessening as my conscience took control. I could do this. I could take care of Lotte and keep my emotions in check.

I found her where I had left her, in the chair. "What can I do for you? Can I make you some tea?"

"No thank you. But I would like to lie down and rest. Would you mind carrying me to my room?"

"It would be my pleasure." I picked her up as she wrapped both her arms around my neck. I so wanted to kiss her. I took her upstairs and headed down the hall toward her room, battling my emotions every step of the way.

I had never been in her room before, not even on the tour Hans had given me. This was sacred turf.

I stopped at the closed door.

She pushed it open.

I peered inside. The room was large with a four-poster bed against the interior wall. Several trunks and a dresser lined the walls.

The large cello case in a corner leaning against a music stand caused me to take a half step back. My gut churned with thoughts of her leaving.

She grabbed my chin and forced my eyes back to hers. "What's wrong? I saw your eyes, staring at my cello. Are you thinking about Pa sending me to the Amsterdam, to the university?"

"Yes."

"If that does happen, it probably won't occur until sometime next year, if then. Pa doesn't have the money. I don't have a place to stay. He just wrote his brother to see if I could board with him and his family. That answer alone will take months. I must apply to the university. All that will take time. If I do go it will be at least a year from now. And many things can happen in a year. Now, please, take me to my bed."

As I bent to lay her on her bed, she held on to me, pulling my face down to hers.

"Lotte, I don't think—"her lips met mine blocking my words.

This time it wasn't a disrupted peck. It was a long, soft kiss with her mouth owning mine.

In an instant, I thought my already pounding heart would explode. My breathing accelerated to a gallop as all the warmth in my body raced south.

She kissed away my Hans-induced guilt, and I eased my body down on top of her being careful not to touch her ankle.

She moaned. Then I felt the tentative brush of her tongue.

Not sure of what I was doing, I copied her actions; my tongue finding hers.

I had never experienced anything like this. She had to be able to feel me growing against her abdomen.

My conscience had lost the control battle when she began kissing me. I didn't try to move.

Her hands left my neck and slid down my back, cupping my butt cheeks and pressing me hard against her.

And it was my turn to moan, "Oh, Lotte."

Grasping the side of my hip, she rolled me off her.

With her pale eyes fixed on mine she took my free hand and placed it over her smock-covered breast.

I wasn't sure what to do. I had never touched a woman's breast before. My fingers explored the contours as well as the hard, little button protruding through the soft material of her gown.

Our breathing seemed to fill the room.

As I fondled her breast, she dropped her hand to the top of my breeches and began unbuttoning them.

When she undid the last button, she leaned down and kissed me. A pounding heartbeat later, she slipped her tongue into my mouth and her hand inside the flap of my trousers, touching me.

My body jerked. I gasped.

And then as soon as her fingers began exploring, my adolescent-accumulated fantasies exploded.

After my breathing returned to normal, I pushed up on my elbows. "I, I'm sorry, I've never been with a girl be——"her finger bridged my lips.

"I understand," Lotte said, sitting up. "I have never been with a boy or a man before either. My mother and I never had a chance for a mother-daughter talk." She leaned down and kissed my cheek. "We both have a lot to learn." She stroked my hair. "I want to learn with you. There is something about you. I don't know how to explain it. You are all I think about. I dream about running away with you."

"Me too. Every time I see you, I feel like I'm floating in air. I have trouble concentrating at work because of you." My conscience returned from wherever it had been shut-in, screaming in my head about control. I pushed up, pulling away from her soothing hair-stroking fingers, and leaned against the headboard. We needed to slow down. Also there was so much I didn't know about her. I touched her cheek. "It must have been difficult for you to lose your mother. How old were you?"

"I was seven. We hadn't been here very long. This house wasn't finished. I had no friends, just Pa. Ma got sick and . . . and everything happened so fast." Her eyes became glassy, and she looked away. "Then she was gone, forever. I didn't think I'd ever stop crying."

"I'm sorry." I reached out and wiped a tear that escaped onto her cheek.

"What about you?" she asked, looking at me.

"What?"

"It had to be hard for you to leave your family." Her wet eyes studied me.

I nodded.

"Is that your answer, just a head nod?" she asked, blinking away her emotions.

I avoided her stare, looking away. "It's something I don't like to talk about."

"Your dad was home. You had a good job, a journeyman. I don't understand why you decided to leave and come to a place where there was a war going on and you knew no one. It doesn't make sense to me, unless . . . was there a girl involved?"

"No," I said emphatically, not wanting her to think there had ever been anyone but her in my life.

Then I realized she had given me a window to escape through. An excuse she could probably accept with Scotland being so far away.

I had never told anyone about the horrible day that had forced me to leave. It was too ugly to share. I didn't want Lotte to know. The risk was too great. The truth might drive her away.

However, I couldn't use her window. I couldn't lie to Lotte. I wouldn't, ever.

This moment had to eventually happen.

A long sigh pushed past my lips.

Chapter Thirty-Four

The day's light was fading through the window in Lotte's bedroom. Semi-dressed, I lay against the headboard of her bed with her sitting up next to me, staring intently into my eyes.

"Then if it wasn't a girl who made you leave your family and career, what was it?"

"Do you have any secrets; things you've never told anyone?"

Finally, she averted her eyes, looking up and to the side. Seconds passed before she fixed on me again. "Our kiss. Pa and I swore we would always tell each other everything. But I never told him about that. I, I should, but . . ."

"I understand." I took her hand in mine. "I've never told my family why I left home. Like you, they were baffled. My parents never accepted my excuse that I wanted to start my own business versus being a journeyman working for someone else for the rest of my life."

"That sounds like a very good reason. That's why Pa came here."

"He told me, but that wasn't my reason, that was an excuse. He tells me everything. And I don't reciprocate. I fear if I tell him or you why I came here, especially you," I squeezed her hand, "neither of you will ever see me henceforth as you do now."

"But, Hamish, as Pa always says you cannot build a relationship founded on secrets. And I so want a future with you in it, as does Pa. We've all made mistakes. You must trust in our understanding of yours."

"And I want to be a part of your future. It's just such a horrible story."

She squeezed my hand. "Tell me."

I pushed up a little taller against the headboard. "As you know, when my father left, I started working for ol' man MacDonald when I was ten. I was a tall kid, but very skinny and weak. None of my family got much to eat back then."

She squeezed my hand, but didn't interrupt.

"The gun shop was eight blocks from where I lived. Aberdeen, like most large cities, had many different elements of people. Some who lived off the sweat of others. Shortly after I began working, on a payday, I encountered such a person on my way home, Bruce, Bruce MacKinnah. Bruce was three or four years older than me and much bigger and stronger. He took my money, but not without a fight. Though I was small, I made him earn it. I still carry the scars, but he never bothered me again."

I took a few seconds to think about how I would explain what had happened to me.

"I learned from both the pain and the fight. Either the rage from being threatened, or the anger, or maybe the fear, I don't know, but something caused me to change when I was endangered. It was as if I became a different person. There were many times after Bruce when it was either fight or starve, and my family never starved." I bent my head and blew out a deep breath, gathering myself.

"Last year, right after the schools closed for summer, on payday, I was cutting through an alley on my way home. A big man named Roderick Campbell stepped out from behind a pile of cobblestones used to repair the street. He blocked my way. He had his little brother James in tow. All of us workers knew of Roderick. He was blessed with muscles, but scorned with the virtues of the Devil."

"We bar our doors and windows because of both the Indians and men like that," Lotte said, her eyes wide. "They are here as well. Please, continue."

"It's all so vivid to me; like it was yesterday." I shook my head. "I asked Roderick what he and his brother were doing in my part of town since he was from the south side. His chuckle faded into a sneer. 'You know why I'm here, MacCardle.' He motioned over his shoulder. 'I brought James 'cause it's time he learned how to provide for himself. So I guess a journeyman like yourself would say this is James' apprenticeship.' He belly-laughed, slapped his bother on the shoulder, and then pushed James behind him. 'You have a reputation for being quite a fighter. But you must know you will not win a tussle with me. And I *will* hurt you. Now why don't you give me your money so I won't have to teach the boy the ugly side of this business.' I attempted to talk him out of trying to take my money but he wasn't going to leave without it."

It was as if I were there again. I felt a calmness ease my grip on her slight hand.

"There was no way I was going to give him my money, and he knew it. 'Unlike me, me brother James is small so I must show him the tricks of the trade.' He reached behind him and pulled out a long knife. 'Now give me your money, or I'll cut that pretty face of yours.' Swinging his knife-holding hand back and forth, he took a few steps closer to me. I instinctively reached for my knife, but it wasn't there. I had let my little brother borrow it. I glanced around for a weapon and the only thing I saw were the cobblestones. I grabbed one and retreated a few steps. I remember the stone being smooth and heavy. Roderick chuckled and closed the distance between us. Cocking my arm, I warned him not to take another step toward me. He smiled and then ran at me. I hurled the stone with all my might at his head. He ducked and the missile thumped like it had hit a pumpkin when it slammed into James' head. The boy collapsed like his legs were suddenly boneless."

Lotte gasped.

I opened my mouth to continue, but her reaction and the emotions of that day were upon me in an instant. My voice failed me. My eyes seared. I took an unsteady breath and swallowed down the relived horror and found my voice again. "Roderick slid to a stop, turned, and rushed to kneel next to his brother. Blood gushed from a wound in James' forehead and his eyes stared into space. Roderick shook his non-responding brother. Then he bolted to his feet, his squinted, watery eyes focused on me. I'll never forget his words. 'You've killed him, you bastard!' He flexed his fingers around the handle of the knife. 'Now I'm gonna cut your head off.' His face contorted into a scream, and he charged me."

Lotte's hand flew to cover her mouth.

"Roderick had lost control. I hadn't."

I took a deep breath. "I know this may sound crazy, but there's this thing inside me. It's like I have a totally different person living inside me. Whenever I'm threatened, another person within me is given life and takes over; a calm and yet violent person. I have trouble understanding it, but it happens. A person I had met before at times like this; someone I had seen in others and despised."

I shook my head. "Anyway, this calm person sets my feet. And when Roderick slashed his knife at my face I hopped back. When the knife swished past my cheeks, I lunged forward. My right hand pinned Roderick's knife-wielding hand across his body and my left fist crushed his charging nose." An involuntary shudder ripped through me.

I didn't realize I was still holding her hand. Without taking her eyes from mine, she pulled my quivering fingers to her mouth and lightly kissed each of them.

"There's more," I said in a weak voice.

"You've kept this ugliness buried too long; let it all out."

I looked away, envisioning that day and all the horrible details.

"This is all so strange. It's as if I were standing back watching the fight rather than being a part of it. When Roderick fell backwards, this thing inside me, this monster, stomped Roderick's knife-holding hand until the broken bones released the blade. This animal, that looked like me, calmly kicked the weapon away, and then was on Roderick, pounding his face with both fists until he was unconscious."

My gaze returned to her. "And as soon as the threat was conquered, I, the man you know or thought you knew, came back. I bolted to my feet and ran to James. I had seen lifeless eyes before, but . . . I felt for a pulse and there was none. I had killed a little kid, no older than my younger brother. Breathless and shaking, I staggered to the wall of the alley and threw up everything inside me, including a chunk of my soul. I knew then I would never be the same."

I studied her concerned face. "I've tried to run away from what I did, but can't. James' staring eyes have haunted me ever since; at times when I least expect it." I sighed. "I . . . I am not the person you think I am." I bowed my twitching head and wept.

Chapter Thirty-Five

The shadows in Lotte's bedroom had grown longer and darker, helping me hide my tear-streaked face. I sat with my head in my folded arms, my back pressed against the pillow-covered headboard of her bed.

There was movement close to me. A single foot thumped on the wooden floor again and again. The surrounding blackness vanished with the striking of a flint followed by flickering candlelight.

More thumping as clothing rustled, and wood scraped the floor. The silence hung in the air for a long moment. Then the room was filled with sound that was foreign to my ears and yet so soft and warming, lifting my wide-eyed head.

Lotte, sitting across the room from the bed, was playing what looked to be an oversized guitar. She cradled the long stem of her cello between her shoulder and neck. Her fingers danced across the stem strings as her other arm slid the bow across the strings at the body end of the instrument.

I had never seen or heard anything like it.

The soft, quick-paced notes climbed, then descended, then rose again. The notes vibrated within me, causing my finger to pat the bed in time with the music.

Lotte had captured my attention, pulling me away from the past.

She became one with her instrument as if it were a part of her. The fingers of one hand caressing the strings as the other stroked them, producing note after note that made my body sway with the rhythm.

Lotte had become someone else. Someone I didn't know. Her beauty, more radiant than ever before, gleamed in the candlelight. The music flowed not just from the cello but from her; an outpouring of passion.

I, the journeyman gun-maker, felt small in her presence. My skills were crude and rudimentary in comparison.

Hans's dream had come to life before me. Lotte had a gift. I now understood why he was so focused on sending her back to the Amsterdam to study music at the university level.

Lotte was in a different world; her world. She had allowed me to enter this place of beauty she had created.

A shiver of astonishment tainted by fear coursed through me.

The bouncing, beating tones swirled up and down around me, over me, through me, again and again.

I didn't want the music to end, but it did. The resulting quiet seemed heavy.

Lotte stared at the floor.

"You must go back . . . back to the Amsterdam." My words were soft and hushed as if I had tried to keep them inside but couldn't.

Lotte stood and, using the wall for balance, hopped the cello back to its stand in the corner of the room.

Then she maneuvered to the bed. "Pa always says my music makes him happy. Did my music make you happy, Hamish?"

I gazed up into her eyes. "Oh yes. You are unbelievable. I know nothing about music, but that was so beautiful, so alive. What's it called?"

"Bach's Cello Suite Number One in G Major."

I studied her as if I had just met her and then looked away. She was so beyond me. I slid my legs off the bed, buttoned my pants, and stood.

"What are you doing?"

I grabbed another candle and lit it off hers. "I'm going to my room."

She shook her head in disbelief.

Warm fingers combed through my hair, waking me. When I looked up I gasped, losing my breath. Lotte, naked, sat next to me.

How she got down the steps and undressed without waking me should have baffled me, but those were discussions for another time.

"Hamish, you are everything I thought you were and more. You're smart. You're strong. But most of all, you care. Pa and music were my life, but now there is you." She leaned down and kissed me.

Lotte stayed with me.

In what seemed to be a long night that went too fast, my life changed. It was if I were Columbus discovering a whole new world.

We explored each other physically, touching, tasting, probing; all leading to us being joined. After a few fumbling and yet wonderful attempts, we climbed the mountain, arriving at the peak together, in a loud, passionate, release.

During our times of recovery, we talked. We questioned each other about our childhoods, our families, what we liked and didn't like, our happy times and sad times, our hopes and dreams, and our strengths and fears.

When dawn's first light cast its outline on the wall of my room, we were intimate both physically and mentally.

I felt older, as if my youth were now behind me.

I cuddled Lotte until she fell asleep. At that moment, I knew she was my world, and I never wanted to be without her.

I was floating, suspended by bliss. I had never been happier, never. Not just because of all my fabulous enlightenments, but also because I knew she felt the same way about me as I did her.

However, sleep evaded me, pushed aside by her dreams as well as her father's.

I could not, would not, be the reason for her not to pursue her love of music.

But how could I live without her?

Chapter Thirty-Six

Hens cackled in the barn. I awoke cuddled with a sleeping Lotte in my room. It hadn't been a dream.

I eased out of bed. Then I took a moment to study Lotte curled up in the blanket, so lovely and at peace, my woman. This had to be a fantasy.

Joy coursed through me from my toes to the tips of my hair. It wasn't a dream. I smiled. If I only had a year with her, so be it. It was a year.

After I dressed, I left on light feet to make breakfast. I glanced out a slit in the back window. It had to be mid-morning. Lotte and I were both burning up sun light. There was much to be done.

I had watched Lotte cook enough to know where she kept all the tools and makings. I started a fire. Then I placed two sets of dishes, forks, and knives on the table.

I found a pan to collect eggs from the chicken coop in the barn when Lotte called from my room, "Hamish? Hamish, where are you?"

Her voice sounded different than it had on previous mornings; softer, more endearing.

"I'm in the kitchen, my love. Making you breakfast," I answered.

"What time of day is it?" she asked.

"Close to mid-day," I said and chuckled.

"Oh my." She hopped on one foot to the door of my room. Dressed in a loose-fitting nightgown, she looked at me.

"You need to quit hopping around before you do more damage to your leg."

"I can fix breakfast."

I laughed as I walked over to her and picked her up. "You cannot cook hopping on one foot."

She leaned into me, wrapped her arms around my neck, and kissed me, a soft, lips only kiss. She pushed back and looked into my eyes. "I would love to skip breakfast and take you back to bed. But . . ."

"I know, duty calls." I carried her into the kitchen and eased her onto her good foot next to a chair. In the bright light from the window I had opened at the rear of the house, I looked into her pale blues eyes and squeezed her against me. "There is much to do. The first being to make you breakfast, tend to the animals, and then make you a crutch. After that I promised your father I'd make at least one more of our new rifles before he returned."

She pouted her lips. "No wonder my father loves you almost as much as I do." She pecked my lips.

Her words about her father stirred my guilt until she added that she loved me. A surge of warmth erased all my other thoughts. She loved me. Her loving me was all that mattered.

I whisked her up into my arms and sat her on the kitchen chair.

I scooped up the pan. "I'll be right back. I'm going to get some eggs." I walked to the back door and removed the bar. I opened it, took one step out and stopped, dropping the pan. "Oh, dear God, I . . . I don't believe it."

"Hamish, what's wrong?" Lotte asked.

Before I could clear my befuddled mind to help her, she had hopped to the back door.

Hanging upside down from a large limb of one of the old oaks in the back yard was a large doe, gutted with its throat cut. Blood had puddled in the grass beneath it. There was a gunshot wound on its flank; Lotte's deer.

Chapter Thirty-Seven

Six days later
Late afternoon

Lotte and I sat in the carriage at the town center waiting for the stage from Fort Reading. I couldn't take my eyes off her. Her cheeks were so rosey and her smile so full of life. She glowed.

She touched my arm. "Hamish, you've got to stop. You can't be looking at me like this when Pa gets here."

"Then you need to cover your face. For if I see it, I can't help but be in awe. Your face is so beautiful and . . . and it tells everything we've done."

She covered her face with her hands. "Oh, no. Tell me you're teasing."

I laughed.

She smacked my arm. "This isn't funny. I've never been able to hide anything from Pa. He knows me better than most ministers know the Twenty-Third Psalm."

I regained control. "Then you'd better think of something sad to change your appearance, because right now you're beaming."

"I don't want to think of anything sad. I want to be happy to see Pa."

"That's a great idea, just think about seeing your Pa and nothing else."

She hit me again.

My thoughts of how to respond were swept away by the pounding of many horses' hoofs approaching.

Around a corner a block away, came five military horsemen, followed by the stage which was trailed by Hans's wagon and two more soldiers on horseback.

Two of the leading horsemen were missing their hats, both had bandaged heads. Another had an arm in a sling.

A low mummer went through the gathered crowd awaiting the coach.

I turned to see Lotte's reaction. She didn't need to worry about beaming anymore.

The stagecoach had several arrows sticking in the sides and only one driver without a guard.

Chapter Thirty-Eight

Lotte and I climbed out of the carriage. I hugged her trembling body against me as we waited for the stagecoach to stop.

"Whoa!" the driver called pulling the reins back against his blood splattered shirt.

"What the Hell happened out there, Frank?" a man in the crowd called to the driver as he set the brake.

Frank, jaws set in a grimace, climbed down from the driver's seat. "Poor, Charley, I always thought if anything bad happened it would happen to both of us." He shook his head.

"Pa!" Lotte screamed as she broke from my grasp and limped hastily to Hans's wagon.

Hans was driving his supply wagon. He was hatless, covered in dust, and had puffy, dark circles under his eyes seemingly being pulled down by his sagging jowls.

Seeing Lotte, Hans clamored off the wagon just in time to be wrapped in a hug from his sobbing daughter.

"Oh, Daddy, are you alright?" She pushed back and looked into his eyes. "Are you hurt?"

"I am fine, sweet girl. Just tired. And what has happened to you, why are you limping?" Hans looked at me for an answer.

"I am so glad you are fine, sir," I said, grabbing his extended hand. "Obviously there is much to talk about. You take Lotte home in the carriage, and I'll see to your luggage and the wagon."

"Thank you, Hamish, but maybe I should unload my wagon and bring it home."

"You take your daughter home, sir, I can handle it."

Hans glanced at Lotte and then turned back to face me. "Besides the fifty British muskets in the wagon that you need to take home, there are four bodies that must be unloaded. That is not yours to do. And please stop calling me sir."

Lotte bowed her head.

"I'll take care of it, Hans," I said.

He patted my shoulder. "It is so good to be here. I did not think I would—"his gaze moved to Lotte again. "Then you take care of it, Hamish. We will talk at home."

The three of us sat at the kitchen table with Hans nursing some home-distilled whiskey a neighbor had given him years ago.

I had just finished telling Hans the story about Lotte's leg and how we had a smokehouse full of venison.

"That's an incredible story. I cannot believe any of those savages have a heart."

"The man could have killed us both, Pa," Lotte said.

"I don't understand why he did what he did, but Hamish you should have killed him after he freed Lotte," Hans said coldly. "There would be one less savage to deal with."

My chin dropped to my chest, and I cupped my mouth with my fist as I looked up at Hans. "And one less deer for us to eat." I dropped my hand to the table and raised my bowed head. "Tell us about your trip, Hans."

Hans took a sip of the whiskey.

"I had a great visit with Lieutenant Colonel Conrad. He was happy with my repairs on his muskets. He paid me, and gave me fifty more Brown Bess muskets to work on. However, I could not interest him in our new gun. But several of the locals at the fort were interested after I gave them a demonstration. They were a little shocked at my asking price of nine versus the normal six pounds. But they obviously thought our gun was worth the price because I received twenty orders with a thirty percent down payment. So the good news is I came back with over two hundred pounds, a bloody fortune."

"Fantastic, Pa, but if you came back without a penny I'd be happy just to have you home," Lotte said.

Though I was happy for Hans, I held my comments thinking the money just brought Lotte closer to leaving. "What happened to you on the way home?"

"We left Reading at sunup; five people in the coach; four men and one woman. Ten mounted soldiers accompanied us. The trip is no more than twenty miles. We should have been here no later than one o'clock. Thank God our military boys were smart. They had a scout riding in front of us. The Indians had cut down a tree blocking the road in a section of woods. The scout came back and told us we needed to find a new route around the possible trap. Good thing, he saved us from being massacred. Though it took us a while, we found a section of hill that had been cleared by what looked to be a flood and could be traversed by the coach and wagon. We circumvented the forest, getting back on the road in a large meadow. We had not gotten into the wheel ruts when mounted Indians came riding out of the trees into the clearing like a swarm of bees, forty or fifty of them."

"Oh dear," Lotte said with her hand to her mouth.

"We must have been at least a mile in front of them; but there was no way we could outrun them. Frank, the coach driver, yelled for us to stand and fight in the open; the clearing was our only chance. We left the woman in the coach with the four armed men. A few of the soldiers unhitched and tied up the horses. The rest of us got in the fort-like wagon. We removed the canvas top and loaded the extra muskets I had."

"How many of our new guns did you have?" I asked.

"All five. I hadn't sold any because of the demonstration we had scheduled here. And they came in very handy. When the Indians got within three hundred yards, I started shooting and hitting them. Five shots, five less Indians. The men were impressed. As I shot, the soldiers would reload as I had instructed them earlier. Five more shots and five more hits caused the Indians to stop about two hundred yards out and take cover in the grass bordering the road. Ten of them rode left and another ten rode right. Moving targets are more difficult to hit at a long distance, but I got a couple of them."

I patted his shoulder. "We made a fine gun, Hans. And you're a great shot."

"I've had plenty of practice as have you."

Lotte scooted forward in her chair. "What happened next?" she asked impatiently.

"The Sergeant yelled that the mounted savages were going after our horses and commanded the three men who had tied them up to guard them. Shortly thereafter, we were attacked from all sides and everything was a blur. It became survival. What seemed like days later, the close to thirty Indians remaining hopped on their horses and rode away. And we limped home. We had lost Charley who fought like a Viking, Mr. Sims, a fine man who had ridden with me on the wagon, and two very brave soldiers, along with several horses." Hans reached across the table, his eyes wet with emotion, and grabbed my arm. "In both my judgment as well as several others', our new Pennsylvania long rifle saved us."

"That pleases me to have helped to save you," I said.

His solemn face flashed a hint of pride. "Trust me, this story about our gun will be told over and over throughout the region. So we need to be prepared. We have much work to do. Speaking of which, what have the two of you been doing other than trying to get my daughter killed?"

Chapter Thirty-Nine

The fading sunlight touched the three of us, Lotte, Hans, and I sitting at the kitchen table. My mind wanted to answer Hans's question about what had we been doing in his absence, but my mouth wasn't cooperating.

I stood. "La-la-let me show you." I turned and walked on shaky legs into my bedroom. I closed the door and caught my breath. What was I supposed to do; tell this father-like-man I'd been sleeping with his daughter since he left? A diversion was my only means of not lying to this man I loved.

A moment later I walked out with a long object wrapped in a cloth. I stopped in front of Hans. "Besides making another two of our guns, I made something special just for you. It's my way of thanking you for bringing me here." I handed him the cloth-wrapped surprise.

Hans's pale eyes sparkled as he took my gift. "It's heavy," Hans said laying the present on the table. "What have you done? I feel like a child at Christmas."

"Aye, you are supposed to," I said.

Hans stood and slowly unwrapped my work.

"Oh my Lord, I have heard of these but I have never seen one, an over-under musket! Did you make this?" He shouldered the gun and sighted down the barrel.

"Aye. Ol' man MacDonald taught me how to make them. We only made a few, and they were nothing like this one. This weapon has two of our barrels over and under. Pull that lever and rotate the barrels."

Hans swiveled the barrels. "That is smooth. You are such a craftsman, Hamish. This is a beautiful weapon and both barrels have our mark on them."

"Look at the stock." I pointed.

"You have engraved my name in the wood." He shook his head and rapidly blinked his eyes. "I have not received a better gift in my life except for my wife giving me Lotte."

"I think you will like it even better after you shoot it," I said. "With our small bore, I thought I could increase the turns of the rifling. So I experimented. This weapon has at least another fifty yards of accuracy. And two shots are always better than one."

"This gun and two more in a week, you must not have had time to sleep." Hans sat the gun down and hugged me.

Normally, a hug from Hans would have warmed me though and through. But as I stared at Lotte over Hans's shoulder, I was a man drowning in a sea of guilt.

Forty

After a long night in which I slept by myself for the first time in a week, and slept poorly, I stood in the shop with Hans.

"Hamish, let's plan on a public demonstration after we finish at least three more long rifles. That will give us thirteen. I think we will be able to sell them after we show the town our new guns. Let us make these next three with your improved rifling, and we will ask ten pounds for them versus nine for the others. We will see who wants to pay more for longer range coupled with accuracy."

"That sounds like a sound plan, but that's a very high price."

"By the time our competition starts to make a similar weapon, which they will, we will have lowered our costs to make these weapons. Then we will lower our prices below what they can make the weapon for. But right now, we are the only gun makers with long range accuracy. So if they want it they will have to pay for it."

"You are quite the businessman, Hans; one step ahead." I glanced away. "It's just that I was thinking of those poor people who have moved out in the wilderness to try to make a living. They are the ones who need this weapon the most."

"If the Indians want to eliminate those people, I doubt our gun will help them." He patted my back. "You have a good heart, Hamish. But those people knew the risks when they moved to the wilderness. It is crazy to be out there even in a small community with this war going on." Hans motioned. "Now you go set up a target at three hundred yards while I start the forge. I want to see how well my new gun shoots."

After firing both barrels of his new gun from the fixed stanchion, Hans and I examined the foot-diameter sap-blackened target on the stump. The ball holes were within the circle and also within six inches of each other.

Hans slapped my back. "Hamish, you are a genius. The additional spiraling along with the sights at each end of the barrels makes such a big difference. I love my new gun. Thank you, again."

"I'm the one who is thankful. I've never been so happy. I just wish this war wasn't going on."

"I agree. And I hate to say this, but this horrible war will greatly increase our sales." He hefted his weapon onto his shoulder. "Let's go make some guns, son."

How could I ever tell a man who called me 'son' that I had violated his trust with his most valued possession, his daughter?

Forty- One
Three Weeks Later
Mid-day

Hans and I were working on rifling a pair of barrels we had made that morning, when Lotte burst into the shop. Her cheeks were crimson as if she had been running.

"Pa, I was in town shopping for supplies, and the stagecoach arrived. Frank was the driver. He saw me and called me to him. I've never seen him so excited. "

"I cannot remember ever seeing Frank excited," Hans said.

"I have," Hamish said, remembering the horrible time all the Indians were chasing the young boys. "But go on, Lotte, finish your story."

"He told me he had been in Philadelphia three days ago, and the talk of the town was your new gun."

"Now I am getting excited," Hans said, smiling. "Continue girl."

"Apparently one of the first owners of our long rifle took his new purchase to Philadelphia and did a demonstration. And look what Frank gave me." She held out a bundle of letters. "There must be at least fifty personally sealed letters from individuals requesting your long range muskets. And he said at least three-hundred more are forthcoming."

Hans shook his head and wiped sweat from his brow. "We are already behind on the near two-hundred orders from our local demonstration. Maybe I was wrong to reduce the price to eight pounds."

"That lower price doubled our business," I said. "It was a wise decision."

"But all these additional orders, we are swamped now." Hans shook his head.

"We aren't that far behind, Hans. Since you decided to pay the Schaefers to make our stocks, we've reduced our workload to making barrels, ramrods, and cleaning tools."

"Yes, and we are still behind."

"We'll be fine, sir. Now that all we have to do is assemble and test fire the weapons, we are going to make close to fifty guns this month."

"But with these new orders, we will have over five-hundred guns to make. That will take almost a year at fifty per month."

"With the new production tooling we're having made, we should be able to make at least seventy-five guns next month, maybe a hundred. And I plan on having the fifty British muskets in working condition by then as well."

Hans patted my shoulder with his beefy hand and nodded. "You make good points, as usual, Hamish. We should be fine. I am just nervous. I want to keep all my customers happy."

"They will love our new gun. It's the best rifle ever made."

"I could have never done this without you, Hamish. You work harder and smarter than any two men I know." A smile squeezed his pale blue eyes to slits, creasing his round face.

"I appreciate that immensely, Hans."

Hans grabbed Lotte's hand and patted it. "Thanks to you, Hamish, Lotte will be able to go back to the Amsterdam sooner than we had planned. She will be able to further her musical education and to live her dream. And the best part is she will become independent and not have to come back to this God-less place. Though I will miss her every second, nothing could ever make me happier."

Lotte and I exchanged glances. My insides burned like I'd swallowed a hot coal.

Chapter Forty-Two

The following week, Hans came back from town where he had picked up the mail from the midday stagecoach. Beaming a smile, he had waved a paper in his hand. "I have great news. This is a letter from my brother in Amsterdam saying not only did he have room for Lotte to board with him, he has a friend at the university. His friend is a professor in the music department who had heard Lotte play as a child. He recalled how gifted she was. He said he would try to get her enrolled by this Michaelmas term and save us all the time it would take to send the enrollment paperwork to us and for us to return the papers and wait for word of acceptance."

"But Pa, I cannot be ready to go that soon, plus you don't have the money and—"

"Thanks to Hamish, I will have the money. Frank gave me at least three-hundred additional orders for our guns. I . . . I did some figuring on the way home." He hesitated to wipe a tear off his cheek. "Lotte, if you are accepted, you will need to leave here before we receive word of your acceptance. You must depart no later than five weeks from now."

Another week had slid by as had another quiet breakfast. Very little was said between us since Hans's announcement. None of us had challenged the ensuing silence. I assumed Lotte and Hans were as troubled as I by the rapidly approaching sadness.

Hans and I were stacking the newly assembled and tested rifles inside the house. For defensive purposes all the rifles were loaded.

"Hamish, we have some deliveries to make, forty-five to be precise. I suggest one of us stays here and continues production while the other exchanges these rifles for money due us."

This was perfect for I needed to talk to Lotte without Hans present. I had thought about what I would say. I would tell her I was happy she was going to live her dream. And in four years, I'd only have a few left to finish my indenture. Maybe by then with what Hans was paying me, I'd have saved enough money to return to Europe if she still wanted me to. Or she could come back here if the war was over unless . . . unless her new life had changed her feelings. I would understand. What I wouldn't say to her is that I'd pray everyday that she still loved me, and we'd be together again. "That is your money to collect, Hans, I will stay here," I said, setting a sling of guns on the floor of the spare room upstairs.

"I trust you, Hamish."

My stomach knotted.

"Twenty of these weapons are for men in town; twenty-five are for farmers in the wilderness. I've given the farmers priority despite the date of their orders. You reminded me how they need these improved guns more so than the in-town people."

I nodded but my aching gut kept me from smiling.

"I suggest you deliver the Lancaster guns this afternoon," Hans said. "Then we will go together tomorrow morning to take the others. That trip will take all day."

Just the two of us were going into Indians country. I tried and failed to swallow the lump in my throat. This man had been like a father to me, but of late, he was stepping on my heart and feeding my fears.

"This afternoon you can use the wagon for your deliveries. Tomorrow we will take a packhorse. That way we can at least try to outrun any trouble."

I said nothing, and began counting out twenty-five rifles.

Hans studied me for a moment. The man could read my emotions.

He patted my back. "Don't worry, I have thought this through. We will go to the Hastings place first; they own several mines and are our furthest customer from town. They live close to a small community of miners."

"That wouldn't be George and Martha Hastings would it?" I asked.

"No. It's Joshua and Rebecca Hastings. But his son and his wife and boy have recently moved in with them."

"Joshua, that's the boy's name. They have to be George's parents. I rode here on the stage from Philadelphia with George, Martha, and Joshua. They said they came to Lancaster to help his parents with their mines."

"Makes sense. They ordered five rifles. They must all know how to shoot. Good thing with them being so far away from the fort."

"How far?" I asked trying to control my voice.

"Six or seven miles. But," he held up a hand, "before you get too concerned, I planned the trip with us going there first, because if there is any trouble, we will have twenty-five loaded rifles in addition to whatever we take with us. And the last farm on our route is only a few hundred yards from town."

I nodded though I was thinking about what the Indians had done to the red-headed boy and the British Sergeant.

Chapter Forty-Three

The bottom of the sun was touching the horizon when I returned from delivering twenty weapons to town people. Hans had made sure I had 'change' money when I left.

I had returned with more money than I had ever seen. Minus the down-payments many of the buyers had given us, I had collected over one-hundred-forty pounds. With my history, that much coin made me nervous. So I stopped at the house to give Hans the money before taking the horse and wagon to the barn.

Smiling, Hans poured the contents of my large, bulging money bag onto the kitchen table, covering it.

Lotte, who was preparing dinner, stopped stirring the contents of a pot as she gasped.

"This along with the additional fifty pounds I plan to give you, Lotte, should easily cover all of your expenses in the Amsterdam for four years, maybe more," Hans said. "This week we will make travel arrangements; then all you have to worry about is what to pack." He laughed.

Lotte, hand over her mouth, glanced at me.

I looked from her to Hans. The thought of her leaving hung on me like a lead coat.

Hans followed her eyes. "Yes, it's true. Living your dream probably would not have happened if Hamish hadn't come to help us."

Lotte stepped away from the fireplace. "Pa, take some of this money and pay the soldiers to deliver the rest of your guns to the farmers tomorrow. Please. I don't want either of you going into that wilderness with this war going on. It's too dangerous."

"My dear sweet, Lotte, our military has lost so many soldiers of late, they barely have the numbers to man the towers leaving the fort with but a few soldiers."

"Then hire some men from town," Lotte pleaded. "There has to be hundreds of men here who would do this for less than a pound each."

"I don't trust them," Hans responded with an edge to his tone I hadn't heard him use with Lotte.

This was a conversation I didn't need to be in. "Excuse me, I'm going to put the horse and wagon in the barn."

I was in hanging the harness on a hook, when I head footsteps. I turned and Lotte had entered the barn and was walking toward me.

"Hamish, I told Pa I was coming out here to try to talk some sense into you, since I couldn't talk any into him."

But instead of stopping, she walked right up to me and flung her arms around my neck and kissed me, a long passionate kiss.

She broke the kiss and ran her tongue over her lips. "I thought we'd never be alone together again. I miss us."

I glanced at the barn door. "This is very risky," I said, hugging her.

"Not as risky as you two going into Indian country tomorrow. Tell him you're not going. Maybe your good sense will be contagious; then he won't go either."

"That won't stop him. He's made a commitment to those people. And he's a man of his word. If I don't go with him, he'll go alone."

She stepped out of my arms, shaking her head. "This is all about the money to send me back to the Amsterdam to the university." She withdrew another step and folded her arms across her chest. She looked away. "I'm not going . . . I'm not going away, ever."

"Lotte, what are you saying?" I closed the distance.

Tears rolled down her cheeks.

I wrapped her in my arms. "This is your dream," I whispered with my mouth against her forehead. "You have a gift. You must go."

She pushed back and looked up at me. "Hamish I'm . . . I think I'm with child."

I couldn't find a breath let alone a response. I just stood there limp staring at her for a long moment.

Hans walked into the barn. "Hamish, if you are still going with me, we need to load the rifles into a packhorse sling tonight so we don't have to do it in the morning."

Chapter Forty-Four

The desolate look on Lotte's face made it very hard for me to mount a horse early the next morning.

Most of the little time she and I had risked to talk yesterday was spent with me trying to find my breath after her shocking announcement. We were going to have a child. After a sleepless night, I was still numb.

I wanted to hug this mother of my child and tell her I would take care of her and the baby, but couldn't. Hans was only a few yards away in the barn. My emotions gurgled and ached within me, close to the point of exploding.

This was not the time to be leaving. She needed me. We needed each other. Unspoken words must be spoken; loving, reassuring words. Plans had to be made.

We had to tell Hans.

I could only guess how she must feel. The two fathers in her world venturing into the land of death, from which neither may come back.

"Don't look so sad, girl," Hans said, as he walked out of the barn leading a packhorse with two larges bundles slung over its back. "We will be back for supper."

After he interrupted Lotte and I in the barn last night, Hans and I had packed the twenty-five individually wrapped rifles along with bags of wadding, bullets, and powder horns.

"This is insane," Lotte said with her arms intertwined across her chest to shield the cool morning air. Lotte wagged her head.

Hans pulled her to him with his free arm. "We will be fine, Lotte. We have enough weapons and ammunition to take on a whole tribe of Indians."

"We *will* be back," I said to her, trying to sound as strong as possible. I leaned down and handed Hans's horse's reins to him.

"You take the packhorse, Hamish, and I'll lead. The lead man always needs a free hand; a gun hand."

This was insane.

I trailed Hans as he weaved his way through the dense woods on what once was a deer trail now worn to the width of a wagon. The mines were in the hills beyond the town. And the ore was brought to market on this trail by miners like the ones who worked for the Hastings family.

Any other day, time, or place, I would have had trouble staying awake after a sleepless night. But this morning, I had too many things occupying my mind.

I was going to be a father.

The woods were so thick, that the early morning light barely filtered through the canopy of leaves. My head constantly swiveled from left to right and back again, looking for movement in the dim light, for men, for red men.

I carried one of our new guns slung over my shoulder by a piece of twine I had tied to the barrel and the stock. Hans's two pistols he'd sent to me in Philadelphia were loaded and stuffed in the pockets of my waistcoat.

My one hand held the packhorse's lead rope; the other hand guided the horse I rode; a beast who seemed to not like me.

If we were attacked, all of my guns would be useless. And if Hans made a run for it, there was no way I could stay on this beast without a free hand to hold on to the saddle.

Hans stopped and motioned me next to him.

I tried to stop my mount but went by him, stopping several strides ahead of him.

Hans walked his horse up to me. "First time on a horse, laddie?"

I blew out a breath. "Yes."

"Well, I guess I should have known that." He reached over and patted my mount on her forehead. "Let me introduce you to Rosey. She is the gentlest mare I have ever rode."

"I don't think she likes me," I said, as the black mare shook her head and snorted. "I'm afraid she wants me off her back."

"She senses your fear and therefore she does want you off her back. You need to relax and then so will she. She will follow her head. Tug the right rein, and she goes right; the left, she goes left." He demonstrated with his rein-holding hand. "Pull back and she will stop. Give her free rein and heel-nudge her and she will trot; do it again and she will run."

"If we have to run, how do I stay on her?"

"Move with her. Go up and down with her and lean with her when you turn her. Keep your balance by squeezing her with your knees and shifting your weight in the stirrups."

I sighed and nodded.

"Do you want to take the lead and have me take the packhorse?"

"No," I said mustering all the courage I had.

He grinned and went ahead of me.

Hans's instructions on horseback riding repeated over and over in my head. It all seemed simple enough, unless I needed to make Rosey gallop. I wasn't sure I could stay on the animal's back if she ran.

Rosey, what a stupid name for a horse.

I had to get through this trip. I had get back to Lotte with Hans unscathed; no matter what it took.

"Miss Rosey, my name is Hamish. What say ye, we be friends, best of friends." I patted her neck.

She neighed.

I wasn't sure if it were an acceptance neigh or a rejection. Only time would tell. I tried to relax, but it was very difficult.

The trail was rarely flat, one hill after another closely bordered by trees, too many trees.

Though the morning air was cool, sweat dripped off my forehead and nose.

I had to survive this trip. I had responsibilities now.

My mind wanted to wander, to fantasize about Lotte's and my child. How the baby would look? If it would be a boy or a girl? How I would hold it, and sing it to sleep?

I wanted to yell to Hans and tell him he was going to be a grandfather. But we had to be quiet, and he needed to be told by Lotte and me together.

A plan had to be hatched. Lotte and I must decide how and when to approach Hans. And we couldn't wait very long.

I glanced at the back of Hans's scanning head. The man had trusted me with his most prized possession, his daughter. I had violated his trust. How would I ever be able to get his trust back?

I wasn't sure what he'd do. If I were him, I didn't know what I'd do.

Poor Lotte, home alone with too much to worry about.

I must get through this.

But there were too many trees.

I had to be alert.

Ready to react to anything that threatened us.

I had to stay on this . . . this Rosey, no matter what happened.

Chapter Forty-Five

Hans and I trekked on horseback mile after nerve-jolting mile, up and down hills through the dense forest.

Along the way we startled several animals, a doe, a fox, and a pair of buffalo; but we were the ones startled, immensely so. Reins and lead ropes were discarded and guns came out cocked and shaking. Each time it took me at least another hill before I got my pounding heart back to normal.

Long after my butt had gone numb and the tension unbearable, Hans signaled for us to stop by a flowing creek.

My legs thanked me for getting off Rosey, but I doubted if my knees would ever meet again.

Hans removed a bag attached to his saddle and handed me his reins.

I tied the horses to trees next to the stream so they could drink but not wander off.

I sat down, rifle in hand, on a log by the gurgling water facing the opposite way that Hans faced. My skin tingled. I just knew many eyes had to be watching us. "Thank God you decided to rest. I seriously don't think men are built to ride a horse for very long. How much further is the Hastings' farm?"

Hans handed me something wrapped in muslin. "Here chew on this. It's venison jerky. You will eventually get use to riding. We should be within a mile of the Hastings' place. It is just over the next hill."

"Doesn't this country have any flat ground like Scotland?"

"Scotland cannot be as flat as the reclaimed lands of the Amsterdam. Hills and even trees were rare things to me before coming here. And no, based on what I have seen, flat does not exist in Pennsylvania."

I looked at Hans over my shoulder. He was like a second father to me. He had always told me nothing but the truth. Lotte was with child because of me. It was time for me to be the man Hans thought I was. This wasn't Lotte's problem, it was mine. He had trusted me. "Hans, we need to —"

"Shhhh," Hans said, rising to his feet. "Did you hear that?

I gulped. "What?"

"Listen," Hans said cupping his ears.

Then over the burbling stream I heard in the distance the last thing I wanted to hear; raising the hairs on my neck. "I think that was a gun firing."

"Let's ride, son," Hans said running to the horses.

Chapter Forty-Six

Another gunshot echoed through the thick woods.

The sun was still fresh, low in the sky, and Hans was already mounted; but not I. I was fumbling with a rifle, the reins, the stirrup, and the packhorse rope.

Hans guided his mare next to me and grabbed the packhorse rope from me along with my rifle.

I climbed on Rosey, and he handed me my weapon but kept control of the guns-slung animal. "Stay with me, Hamish. We cannot get separated. I am going to go as fast as this packhorse will let me." He kicked his mount and off he went, through the trees back to the trail.

I slung my musket over my shoulder, grabbed a handful of the front of the wooden saddle with one hand and the reins with the other. "Be kind to me, Rosey." I gave her free-rein and jabbed my heels into her flanks. She almost leapt out from under me, but somehow, I hung on.

As we neared the crest of the next hill, the gunshots got louder, causing more bile to invade my already gurgling, bouncing stomach.

Hans stopped at the top, and I gladly pulled up next to him and patted Rosey's neck.

The valley below us had been cleared of trees. A large two-story wooden house sat in the of the middle of the treeless meadow. There were bodies on the ground outside of the home, two red, one white.

Smoke and flames rose from the rear of the dwelling. A burning brush-filled wagon had been shoved against the back door.

Then I saw movement inside the home. A man and a woman aimed rifles from two separate windows.

I gasped. My first reaction was to race down and pull the burning wagon away. However, the structure was already ablaze, and me galloping on a horse was still a big risk.

Several out-buildings stood behind the blazing home. They had not been torched.

The Hastings would have to make a run to the barn soon.

"I don't see any living Indians," I said, between gulped breaths.

"These Indians are skilled warriors. They are somewhere in the surrounding woods waiting for the fire to drive the Hastings out of the house."

"What are we going to do?" I asked, a little surprised at how calm I had become.

"We need to find out where the Indians are," Hans said, as he scanned the edge of the woods around the house. "That family cannot stay in the house much longer."

I viewed the area. "Over there," I pointed. "See that outcropping of rock halfway up the hill about twenty-yards or so from the edge of the clearing. If I were the Indians, I'd be on that rock."

"Yes. You are such a smart lad."

We headed our horses into the woods in the direction of the rock. When we were within earshot, I stopped.

"Hans, let's leave our horses here and walk with the packhorse," I whispered. "If we can get to that rock, we can probably see most of the Indians from there."

Hans nodded and we dismounted.

Hans lead with his over/under rifle shouldered. I, pulling the packhorse, with a cocked pistol in hand, moved as quietly as possible down the hill through the thick woods.

Thoughts of the Hastings had consumed me up until this moment. Now we were Indian hunting. What if I saw the scar-face red man, Lotte's and my savior? What would I do? If it were Hans or him, I'd have no choice. I sucked in a deep breath.

As Hans stepped to the edge of the tree-line near the rock, the packhorse jumped and neighed.

An Indian with a black mask painted over his eyes and white stripes on his cheeks jumped from behind a tree with his tomahawk raised. His eerie face was enough to send a shiver through me.

Hans aimed.

The attacker dropped to the ground.

Hans adjusted his aim and pulled the trigger, just a click and nothing more; a misfire.

The Indian's contorted face eased into a smile.

Hans spun the barrel, primed the fire-hole, and cocked it as the savage leaped to his feet.

The red man bolted at Hans.

Hans fired at close range, slamming the savage into a tree which he slid down with a look of surprise frozen on his face.

"Nice gun, Hamish," Hans yelled over his shoulder.

The tumult brought another face-painted Indian off the rock, with his rifle raised and aimed at Hans.

There was no time to think. I shot him in the chest. I quickly switched the spent pistol with the other loaded one and cocked it. My hands steady, unbelievably calm.

Hans ran to the packhorse and began opening the pack.

Another Indian with a chilling look came running through the woods. Yelling what had to be a war cry, he fired his musket. Wood chips flew from the tree next to my head, stinging my cheek. Holding my breath, I aimed and fired, dropping him.

Hans carried one of the two bundles of guns out onto the outcropping.

I pocketed the smoking pistol and pulled my musket off my shoulder and cocked it. Behind a tree with my back to Hans, I scanned the woods.

Hans came back and leaned three more muskets against my tree. "Your face is bleeding. Are you shot?"

I touch my cheek and looked at my blood-covered fingers. "I'm fine. It's just a scratch."

He nodded. "You watch my back." He tied the horse to another tree. He took the second cluster of guns onto the rock.

Hans began shooting into the woods below him as fast as he could change one gun for another.

With the three muskets leaning against the elm I stood behind, I faced the woods.

A shadow raced from one tree to another. I braced.

As the figure stepped from behind a broad oak, I shot him; then another and another.

Hans stopped firing long enough to bring me four more guns.

An arrow slashed the air close to me, and Hans groaned.

I risked a glance at Hans. He writhed on the ground trying to reach the shaft protruding from the back of his upper leg. "Be still. I'll be there as soon as I can."

Another feathered shaft sliced the air several feet from me. I thought it was poorly aimed until the packhorse screeched, dropping to its knees.

Thank God that damned thing missed Rosey.

I had four guns. All the rest were on the rock.

The woods in front of me had come to life with movement. Hans and I had obviously gained the attention of all the attacking Indians.

A dark figure darted from one tree to another. I fired and missed; three shots left.

My eyes raced to Hans and then back to the rustling woods. Hans was crawling slowly onto the outcropping.

An Indian's painted face popped out from behind a tree and then withdrew. I almost squeezed the trigger.

They were teasing me. Trying to get me to expend my ammunition. Hans was right about these people; they were battle-hardened smart.

Hans emitted a harsh, loud moan.

His cry forced me to glance at him. Another feathered-shaft stuck out of his upper arm.

With his good arm, he pulled his body behind one of the arrow-protruding bundles.

The woods in front of me erupted in thrashing movement, refocusing my attention.

Two bellowing Indians, tomahawks fisted, sprinted toward me. As I stepped to the side of the tree to aim; the air was filled with slashing arrows whizzing around me. A fire of pain sliced my upper left arm, but somehow I held the gun steady and shot the one closest to me in the head. The second one was on me. I flipped the gun-butt forward and swung it like a club as the red-man swung his hatchet knocking my gun out of my hands. I jumped back, grabbing my knife.

My knife looked so small compared to the tomahawk. I had to swallow a lump of doom in order to focus. For Lotte's sake, I had to save both Hans and the father of my child.

The painted savage glanced at my little knife and smirked. Then he started side-stepping in an arch around me, swinging his weapon back and forth, emitting a guttural, melodic noise.

To Hell with this killer of women and children!

I moved in an opposite direction swinging my small knife, bellowing out the only hymn I knew.

"All hail the power of Jesus' name!

Let angels prostate fall

Bring forth the royal diadem,

And crown Him Lord of all"

His smirk faded into a scowl, and he stopped.

I also stopped and braced.

The Indians raised his tomahawk, shrieked, and took a step—a close-by shot boomed and the savage dropped to the ground.

"I didn't . . . I didn't know you could sing, laddie," Hans said as if each word were an effort, from behind the smoking musket. Then his head dropped below the bundle of guns.

I grabbed the savage's hatchet and jumped back to the tree. I placed both my knife and the tomahawk in my waistband. Then I snatched up and cocked another musket, two shots left.

I checked my burning arm. My slashed shirt sleeve was blood-soaked. I pulled the material away and saw a red gash across the full width of my upper arm. I would have to deal with it later; if later came.

If I were these Indians, I'd send at least three the next time. I picked up the second and last rifle and cocked it. With one in each hand, pressed against my shoulders, I braced them on opposite sides of the big elm.

If I went down, I'd take at least one, maybe two, with me.

A twig snapped to my left, then a leafed-branch swished to my right.

They were moving, enticing me to show myself.

Probably due to fear, maybe for luck, I didn't know, I started singing the hymn again with a shaking voice.

A dry mouth accompanied dreadful thoughts of never seeing Lotte or my child again.

I sang louder.

Halfway through the second verse, my voice cracking, a shot rang out, then another.

A sliver of hope sliced through me. The Hastings had to have come out of the house.

I glanced around the tree, and the Indians were moving away from me. I set one of the guns down and aimed the other at a retreating red form. It was an easy shot, less than a hundred yards. But I couldn't do it. I couldn't shoot a man running away from me.

Another shot boomed nearby and another.

The Indians melted into the trees.

I ran to Hans, hoping I wasn't too late.

Chapter Forty-Seven

The sun was high in the sky when I clambered onto the bloodied rock outcropping and knelt next to the moaning, wounded Hans, laying on his stomach. He looked like a stripped porcupine with not quite all of his quills missing.

"What do I do?" I hesitantly set my gun down. "Shall I pull these arrows out of you?"

"I've," he gritted his teeth, "I've seen some do that and others . . . cut them out or push them through. What ever way used, it wasn't easy." He glanced over his shoulder. "Try pulling the one out of my leg first. It pains me the most and keeps me from walking."

I placed a foot on his calf and grabbed the shaft with both hands. I hesitated.

"Get on with it," Hans said.

I didn't want to hurt him. But I wasn't going to be able to get him off this rock in his current condition. Then I thought of a way to minimize his physical pain. Thank God I couldn't see his face. "I'm in love with your daughter," I blurted and then tugged.

Hans screamed as the arrow came out along with a chunk of flesh and a gush of blood. His head dropped to the ground.

I checked him. His eyes were closed, but he was breathing.

I gently tore his shirt sleeve from his wounded arm. I cut off a piece of the cloth, folded it and placed it over the wound on his thigh. Then I tied the remaining sleeve around his leg, clamping the folded material against the puncture.

A rustling in the woods diverted my attention to the trees. I shouldered my cocked musket.

George Hastings stepped from behind a large maple, hands raised. "Hamish, is that you?"

I lowered my gun, easing out a held breath. "Yes, George, it is I. Thank God, you came." I motioned at Hans. "I could use your help."

George, his face smudged with soot, rushed out onto the rock and wrapped his arms around me.

I just stood there not knowing what to do.

"We, my family and I, are the ones who are thankful." George stepped back and sighed. "We were moments from either being burned alive or massacred when you arrived. You saved us, at least all of us but my father. He was coming in from the barn when the bastards attacked." He took a deep breath as he fought to maintain control. "He didn't make it."

"I'm sorry." I set down my musket and knelt next to Hans. "George, this is Hans Blekkink; my . . . my friend and boss. We were on our way to deliver your gun order when we heard shots. He's been hit in both his leg and arm by arrows. I need your help getting him to shelter. And we need help carrying all these weapons."

George whistled and an elderly woman along with Martha, his wife, and Joshua, his son, came out of hiding. All busily reloading their muskets and warily looking all around them as they approached.

Chapter Forty-Eight

I had killed before, but that was different. Scotland was an accident.

When I killed during the night home invasion attempt by the Indians, that was a blind shooting.

Now . . . now I was a killer.

The sun had just passed it's peak and was on the downhill side of its daily arc.

The Hastings family including the body of the senior Joshua, and Hans and I, along with our recovered horses and guns, were in their barn. The shelter smelled of fresh hay and horse manure.

George and his son, each with one of our new rifles, stood watch at opposite windows.

I began reloading all of the spent muskets as Martha and her mother-in-law, Rebecca, attended to Hans's shoulder wound.

Rebecca stood. "That's all I can do for Mr. Blekkink with what we have." She turned and saw the covered body of her late husband. The crashing of the burning house's roof falling down jerked her attention to the open barn doors where sparks flew. Her chin fell to her chest as a moan escaped. "I've lost everything."

George rushed to her side. "We're here for you, Mom. And we need you, each and all of us. We will get through this God-awful day together." He hugged her. "We love you."

"We do, Grandma," Joshua added glancing over his shoulder.

Joshua looked so much older than he did just a few months ago on the stagecoach. He had a weak moustache and a quiet confidence about him. The adolescent reminded me of a young, chin-raised Scottish lad leaving Scotland, his family and home, for a new world.

Then Joshua's head jerked back to the window. "We've got more company. The men from the mine are here." He rushed to the barn door.

I followed Joshua. Six men, fisting muskets, galloped on horses through the clearing.

"God bless them, they came," George said from close behind me.

He stepped around us and whistled. Then hollered, "Jenkins, we're over here."

Martha came to me and touched my arm. I winced. "You need some attention as well, Hamish. Let me take a look at your arm. We have an herbal salve we use on the horses that is good for open sores."

I looked into her delving eyes and wondered if she was still curious about my past. Her kindness seemed genuine. "Aye. Thank you, I'd appreciate it."

She glanced at Hans whose eyes were closed, resting. "How is your indenture with Mr. Blekkink working? Are you happy?"

She was still inquisitive. I nodded as I held out my arm to her.

She gently cut away my shirt sleeve threads at the seam. "I'll be able to mend this if you wish to save it. But I fear it will be permanently soiled by the blood stain."

"Mending it would be nice," I replied.

I studied her for a moment wondering how much I should share about my personal life with such a curious person.

"I'm very pleased with the indenture. Hans is a good man and an extremely talented gunsmith. We've been very successful as you and your family will discover as soon as you shoot one of our new long rifles. These muskets are very accurate over two-hundred-fifty yards."

"Oh my," she said as she cleaned my wound with a damp cloth. "I pride myself on my shooting skills, but I don't think I could even see that far."

A broad-shouldered dust-covered man in his thirties with a black beard reined a horse in at the opened barn doors. He ducked his head to look into the dark recesses of the barn. "Mr. Hastings, sir, may you and your family all be fine. I began gatherin' some men as soon as I heard the shootin'."

"My father was killed," George said, shading his eyes as he looked up at the mounted man.

"I am so sorry, sir. Is anyone else hurt?" he asked his eyes searching. "I . . . I wish we would have—"

"You did all you could've done, Jenkins. The rest of the family is fine. Father was coming in from the barn when they attacked. There was nothing anyone could have done to save him."

George took a deep breath and released it. "I pray by coming here the six of you didn't endanger the others."

"The ten or so men left have gathered their families and braced for for an attack," Jenkins said. "They'll fight to the death to keep their loved ones and homes safe." His flexed his jaws. "Theys done this before."

He looked down and rubbed his bearded chin. "Everyone out here depends on his neighbors."

"The six of you being here means a great deal to me and my family." George pointed at me. "This young man, Hamish, and his boss saved us. They are gunsmiths from Lancaster who were delivering guns we had ordered. Thank goodness they came when they did. And with their small arsenal, they drove the Indians off. Unfortunately, Mr. Blekking was wounded, but should recover according to his skillful caretakers." He motioned to Martha and Rebecca.

The big man dismounted and walked over to me, his dark eyes reflecting the brownish-orange ore smudged on his cheeks.

"Jeremiah Jenkins, sir." He shook my hand. "It makes me right proud to make your acquaintance."

"Hamish MacCardle." I nodded and released his rust-colored hand. I turned to George. "I've got to deliver the rest of these guns and get back to Hans's daughter. She's alone."

"Well I doubt if Hans can sit a horse with his leg wound, and you can't do that alone. Trust me, you wouldn't get a mile. And Hans's daughter is alone but in Lancaster, she should be safe."

"She expects us back there today. And we are committed to provide our customers with their purchased weapons. I don't have a choice. I'll have to come back for Hans."

Jenkins shook his head. "If you goes out there alone, you'll soon be a dead man."

Chapter Forty-Nine

I stood in the Hastings' barn and the sun wasn't waiting for any of us. If I was going to deliver the rest of the rifles and get home before dark, I had to leave now.

The thought of going back on that trail alone caused my scalp to tingle and my hands to shake. Hastings and Jenkins were right, it was suicide.

We had killed quite a few Indians today and they had to be wanting revenge. I was sure they were watching us, and when I left with all these guns, they'd pick their spot to take me.

I blew out a tension-filled-breath and loaded the slung guns on Hans's horse.

I would have to ride hard. Though Rosey and I were getting to know each other better, I was far from being a good rider. The thought of falling off a galloping horse worried me as much as the Indians did.

Jenkins stepped toward George. "Sir, we ain't goin' back to the mine today, not with the Indians all stirred up. If you wish, my men and I can get some provisions and go with him. If he can put us up for the night, we should be back by mid-day tomorrow."

Halfway into knotting the lead rope to Hans's gun-slung horse, I stopped. He had my attention.

George glanced at me and then at Jenkins. "You're a good man Jenkins and what you say makes sense. But can you promise me you'll get all of these men back here safe and sound?"

Jenkins raised his hands in desperation. How could he promise that?

"George, I'll make sure they get back," I said, cinching the knot and stepping into the conversation. "We will have these extra rifles for most of the way back to Lancaster." I patted the sling. "As I deliver the rifles the numbers will dwindle but so will our distance to the town. When I get home, I'll give each of them two of our new guns for the trip home. That should help them ward off any attack. When I return to get Hans, I'll take the guns home with me."

"That's a sound plan, Hamish," George said. "But you can't come back here alone. You won't make it."

"I'll get some help," I said, though I didn't know who or how.

George nodded at Jenkins. "God's speed."

The thought of going home and being alone with Lotte for a few days made me anxious to leave. Getting there was another issue.

I hated leaving Hans behind, but neither of us had a choice. I pushed thoughts of coming back to this place out of my mind. Other more demanding issues faced me, like going back into those woods today.

Jenkins had gathered his men and provisions, and I had said my good-byes to the Hastings.

Lead rope to Hans's horse in hand, I reluctantly mounted Rosey in their barn. Once in the saddle, my legs didn't feel as foreign as before.

Musket slung over my shoulder and pistols tucked in my waistband, I heel-nudged the mare and moved out of the barn into the open, joining the six others.

Outside the walls of the barn, I knew there had to be Indians watching us. My senses peaked as did the goose-bumps on my arms as we trotted into the woods onto the wagon trail.

Jenkins led, followed by me and the packhorse. The five others trailed me, all of them carrying two of our new loaded guns slung either over their saddle bows or shoulders. They carried their own muskets in hand. I prayed they wouldn't need to find out that carrying their old guns instead of ours was a big mistake.

We were primed and ready. I just hoped the Indians knew it.

The farmers, for their own safety, lived in clusters of at least three families. So we only had three stops to make, with the last one very near Lancaster.

Though we would be without the extra weapons after the last stop, if attacked, we could gallop into town in minutes.

As we moved through the dense, dark forest up and down hills, my mind wanted to drift to thoughts of being with Lotte again, just her and I, alone. However, my survival instincts were too busy checking out each and every tree for Indians.

Palms sweating, head swiveling, if I saw a red man I was committed to being the attacker, to fire the first shot.

By the time we got to the nearest customer, my shoulders were knotted and my shirt soaked with sweat. Being out of the woods, and getting off of Rosey and stretching, was such a relief.

After collecting the money due and politely refusing several supper invitations, we were back into the woods, back to the teeth-grinding fears.

After the second stop, I wasn't sure I had the energy or courage to return to the woods, but I did, we all did.

We arrived at Hans's home with the sun being a small slice on the western horizon. For some reason, whether it be luck or an act of Providence, no Indians had showed themselves.

Fear had consumed my strength. I wasn't sure I could dismount, until I saw Lotte run out of the house.

Chapter Fifty

I had never seen Lotte run before except when she was chasing her wounded deer. This day, months after her ankle injury, she moved like an antelope, grace and adoration in motion. The setting sun made her flowing blonde hair shine.

"Hamish, oh thanks be to God you're back," Lotte said, grabbing Rosey reins. "Your face . . .your arm." Her head quickly scanned the other six mounted men. A panicked look creased her features. "Where is my father?"

I dismounted and hugged her to me. "He's fine, but," I eased her to arm's length, "when we arrived at the first customer's spread, the Hastings, they were under attack from a large force of Indians. Your dad and I distracted the savages long enough to allow the Hastings to get out of their burning home and help us drive the Indians away. Hans got wounded in the arm and leg and couldn't ride a horse. But he's in good hands with the Hastings."

"So why are you here?" she asked.

"I came back because I had to deliver the rest of the guns, and we wanted to make sure you were safe.

Also your dad and I didn't want you to worry about us. I'll be going back for him."

She looked away and grimaced, wringing her hands. "People get infections from wounds. I've seen it. And they can lose limbs or . . . or even die." Her intense eyes returned to mine. "I must go to him and make sure he is well. I must."

"I know the Hastings; your father's in good hands. But we'll discuss it later. First we must make accommodations for these men in the shop, and tend the horses. They volunteered to accompany me. I am indebted to them."

"Have you eaten?" she asked looking at the many men.

"Yes, we had some fresh jerky on the trail, thanks to our last customer. Their horses need fed. What they and their mounts both need is rest. They plan on leaving in the morning. Can you feed them breakfast?"

She nodded.

I took Lotte's arm and walked over to the men.

Jenkins was a big man, a half-a-head taller than me.

"Jeremiah Jenkins, I'd like to introduce you to Miss Lotte Blekkink, Hans's daughter. Lotte this is Mr. Jenkins; he's a foreman at the Hastings' ore mine. And thanks to him and his men, I was able to get back here today."

"My pleasure, Miss Blekkink. I believe me and my men would be without work if Hamish and your dad hadn't arrived and saved the Hastings family." The whole time he talked, his black eyes scanned Lotte in a manner I didn't care for, lingering where they shouldn't.

After the men and I hobbled our horses in the pasture rich with grass, Lotte and I made bedding for the six men in the shop.

Lotte and I bid them a good night and returned to the house.

"Those men . . . they make me uncomfortable," Lotte said, bolting the door.

"They're miners. They're coarse, but I think they're good men. They helped me get back to you." I took her in my arms and kissed her. A familiar warmth surged through me. I broke the kiss before I lost control.

"Lotte, I love everything about you. I can't believe I'm going to be a father. I've never thought about being a dad before. It both scares me and excites me. Let's get married now."

She pushed back out of my arms. "But Hamish, we must tell Pa. I cannot marry you without his blessing and his presence."

"I already told him, sort of."

"You did?"

"I told him I loved you."

"What did he say?"

"Well, I told him just before I pulled an arrow out of his leg. I wanted to divert his attention; take his mind off his leg."

"And?"

"And he passed out. We haven't spoken since."

She folded her arms across her chest and shook her head. "I cannot and will not keep secrets from him. We must tell him everything."

"I agree. I'll go get him and bring him home and then we'll tell him . . . everything." I unfolded her arms and pulled her against me. "Now may I spend the night with the mother of my child?"

A smile creased her lips. "I'd love to spend the night with you. But I'll only do it if you promise to take me with you to get Pa."

Chapter Fifty-One

The next morning, I was in the kitchen making a fire for Lotte. My mind was busy with trying to figure out how to talk her out of going after Hans with me.

A booming knock rattled the back door. I peered through the rifle slit to see Jenkins and his men.

"Good morning," I said, standing in the doorway. "You're a little early for breakfast."

Jenkins along with the rest of his men were each carrying one of our new muskets.

"You boys planning on doing some hunting afore breakfast?" I asked, motioning at their weapons.

With that being said, they each raised their guns and pointed them at me.

Confusion battled my concern as I staggered backwards, arms raised. "What're you doing? Is this a joke?"

Jenkins stepped into the house, his weapon cocked and held waist-high, aimed at my stomach.

The big man's cold eyes made me retreat further into the kitchen.

"You ever work in a mine, Hamish?" Jenkins asked, his voice flat and deep.

I shook my head.

"It's dark, cold, and damp. And the ore dust hangs in the air, makin' it hard to breath. A work day eats the light; ya goes into the mine in the dark, works in the dark, and comes out in the dark. And they pays you little if anything for all the back-breaking labor and awful conditions."

The rest of his men nodded and grumbled agreements as they followed him inside.

"Me and the boys watched you collect more money yesterday than we've ever seen. I figure more money than all of us put together make in a year; a bunch more. That ain't right; it just ain't." He moved his head like he needed to shake something out of his matted hair. "So we decided we want that money along with all the rest you got in this fort of a house."

I stared hard into Jenkins' fierce eyes. "That money isn't mine to give or yours to take."

"Now now, Hamish, don't be gettin' your feathers all ruffled. We know it isn't your money. It belongs to your boss. You're just like us, a servant for the rich." He motioned with the rifle. "Take us to the money, boy." His eyes seemed to get darker. "Or we'll shoot you and take everything worth anything belonging to your boss, including his pretty daughter."

Chapter Fifty-Two

Jenkins and his five men, all aiming muskets at me, had fanned out across the room.

Fear and anger churned in my guts. Fear for what these men may do to Lotte. Anger for my blind trust of men I didn't know.

I couldn't fail Hans; not again.

"Are you going to kill me?" I shouted.

Feet softly patted on the floor above.

"Go ahead and get her down here," Jenkins said with a chuckle. "We'd all like that."

A couple of the other five chuckled.

"She won't come down here. She's smarter than that. And none of you will ever get up those steps. She's a better shot than any of you. And if she does miss, the ricochets off the stone walls will at least wound if not kill anyone on those steps."

"So that's where the money be; upstairs," Jenkins smiled. "Getting up there be a easy problem to fix, Hamish. We just let you lead the way. From what I could tell, she ain't gonna shoot you. Now who's the smart one?"

I dropped my arms to my sides in defiance. "I won't do it."

He stepped closer to me. "You will. If we have to beat you silly and carry you, you will." His contorted, mean face enforcing his words.

"Have you thought this through?" I asked trying to keep my voice calm. "When they catch you, they'll hang you; all of you." I scanned the others. "Is a year's pay worth your lives?"

"I've seen a hangin' once," one of the men said, shaking his head.

"Me too," another said. "I don't want any part of that. They gonna hang us, Jenkins?"

"They won't be lookin' where we's goin'," Jenkins said. He pointed his trigger finger toward the ceiling. "Is there somethin' going on between you and that sweet young thing, Hamish?" He smiled. "We's think there is." He rubbed his chin. "We's all got families too." He motioned to the others. "We ain't animals, we just want to live better. Have a new start in this country, like everyone else whos come here. You's a good lad, Hamish. We don't want to hurt ya. I tell ya what, you take us to the money, and we promise we won't touch that girl. Right boys?"

A few nodded.

"I got a wife," said the one who said he'd seen a hanging. "I'd just as soon go home to my family and forget all this stuff."

"I, ah, I agree with him," said another man with his head bowed; unable to look at Jenkins. He had also spoke about not wanting to be hanged.

"As soon you both touch your share, you'll talk differently," Jenkins said. "No more blabberin'; we're doing this."

I looked at each of the men. They were all physically strong, but whether or not they were men of their word was a guess. At least two of them were not completely committed; at least not now.

I had always fought for my money and this was like mine since it also was Lotte's money. But more than that, our earnings were to make Lotte's and Hans's dream come true.

I didn't stand a chance against six armed men. Or even four if two faltered.

No matter what happened I had to protect Lotte. No matter what. She and my child were worth more than all the money in the world; much more.

But how could I trust Jenkins the way he had looked at Lotte?

Chapter Fifty-Three

"Lotte, take as many muskets as you can carry and bar yourself in the store room!" My voice boomed in the large first floor area of Hans's home.

Jenkins, scowling, took a step toward me.

Feet thudded across the ceiling and then back. A door slammed.

I held up my hands. "I'll get the money for you; all of it."

Jenkins nodded, his dark emotional-less eyes sending a chill down my spine. "That you will."

I led the untrusting bunch upstairs into Hans' room, glad to see Lotte had followed my request and stayed hidden. There I took Hans's chest key from above his back-window sill. Then I opened the chest by his bed and gave them all the money inside; two-hundred-forty-six pounds. I counted it, for I would get every penny back before I was done.

"That's a lot of money, Hamish." He snatched me by the front of my shirt, ripping it. "But be that all?"

I knew Hans had given Lotte one-hundred-ninety pounds a week ago for her trip. So I stretched the truth to a thief; so what. "We labored night and day for months to make that. That's a fortune. Yes, that's all of

Hans's and my money. May you rot in Hell before you have a chance to spend a penny of it!"

He studied my eyes for a long moment. Then he pushed me away. "All right. Carl, get all the mounts from the pasture. Stanislav, go to the the barn, tie all their horses together with a lead rope and bring them to Carl."

He shoved me into the hall. "Which room be the girl in?"

When I hesitated, Jenkins smiled. "I just want to talk to her . . . through the door." He went down the hall, opening doors.

"I wouldn't try to open that one," I said when he got to the storage room door. "You may get shot."

He banged on the door with his fist. "Miss Lotte, I just want to tell ya, I be real sorry not to have gotten to know you better." He chuckled. "But we gotta go. Oh, one ot'er thing, if you go shootin' at us from your winda, we'll kill Hamish. Don't go makin' any trouble for us, and Hamish will come home to ya."

"Please leave Hamish here." Lotte voice was firm though pleading. "I won't shoot at you."

"Just mind my words."

Repeatedly poking me in the back with the musket barrel, Jenkins forced me down the stairs and out the back door to the waiting horses.

Jenkins had the money; now all he had to do was escape with it. I was his only threat. Where was he taking me? And what was he going to do to me?

The thought of possibly never seeing Lotte again etched through my self-control. Each step took me farther and farther away from Lotte and my unborn child.

I squared my shoulders. I was and would be a threat.

They led me, riding bareback on one of Hans's strung-together horses, into the woods, stopping at the trail to the mines.

"You know if you try to follow us your brown hair will end up on some lodge pole," Jenkins said and released me, lowering his weapon and throwing the lead rope at me.

I caught the rope. "You don't know me very well."

He laughed, but his eyes didn't take part.

On the way back to Lotte, my rage grew. No one had ever stole from me and walked away unscathed.

Then the dead boy's eyes returned.

I blinked away the cold vision.

That was about me.

This was about Hans and Lotte.

Hans had been like a father to me. I was indebted to him. And I had just given away his dream money, everything he'd worked so hard for; gone.

I had to get it back.

I was going hunting.

It was mid-morning, when I rode Rosey up to the back of the house.

Lotte ran out of the back door. "Thank God, you're back. Are you all right?"

I dismounted and hugged her. "Yes. They got what they wanted, all two-hundred-forty-six pounds of it."

She gasped.

I stepped back. "At least for the time being."

She eyed me with concern. "What are we going to do?"

"Jenkins and his gang dropped me off at the trail to the mines. Based on what they'd said, I think they are going home to get their families. After that, I have no idea where they'll go."

"At least we know their first stop," Lotte said.

"On my way back, I thought about stopping at the nearest tower and asking for help. But I already knew what they would say. They would've told me I'd had to go to the fort." I shook my head in frustration. "I already know the fort is undermanned now."

She nodded.

"That leaves me with one of two choices," I continued. "I can go into town and see if I can hire some men to either help me go after Jenkins or to retrieve Hans. Or go after Jenkins by myself and then get Hans."

"And if anyone did go with you, could you trust them? You trusted Jenkins and look what happened."

"Precisely." I released a long breath to try to control my emotions. "I've never let anyone rob me; not without paying for it one way or another." Despite my efforts, my emotions painted my words. "And Jenkins and his men will pay."

"I'll change clothes and be ready in no time," Lotte said, with a look of hope on her face.

"Lotte, I'm going alone. I want you to stay with the neighbors. If I don't catch the robbers between here and the Hastings' farm, I'll see if your dad's capable of riding." I stepped past her to take the horses to the barn.

She grabbed my arm. "Remember your promise? I'm going with you."

I looked down into her firm face. "Lotte, if I don't catch Jenkins and his band on the trail, Hans will want to go after them."

"You'll need an extra shooter and a fine one at that."

"We'll have to ride hard to catch the thieves. You're with child; galloping on a horse cannot be good for you."

She set her jaw. "I won't *break*, Hamish."

"It's too dangerous. Besides Jenkins and the other five gun-toting scoundrels, there are many Indians out there."

"All the reasons why you can't go by yourself."

I clenched my teeth and looked away. "I have no choice. Hans will try to come home by himself if I don't get there today."

Her eyes bore into mine. "You promised."

Chapter Fifty-Four

The sun was close to peaking when I rode Rosey onto the dusky mine trail, leading a pack horse with a week's provisions for three and six of our new loaded muskets. The seemingly sky-touching trees on either side of the trail were so thick they blocked the light and the breeze. The air was still and heavy, smelling of pine and rotting vegetation.

Just a few horse strides into the trail and my shoulder muscles were already bunched and my hands wet. My head turning, my eyes scanning, looking for movement.

"Do you think Pa will be able to ride tomorrow?" Lotte asked, trotting her horse next to mine.

Every time I looked at her my stomach knotted. I shouldn't have brought her. This dark tree-canopied trail was too dangerous.

I hesitated to answer her because I knew what her Pa would be capable of regardless of his condition. If by some miracle we got to the Hastings' farm, Hans would be very upset when he saw her. And when he found out we had been robbed, he'd be unstoppable.

Like me, she had two pistols tucked in her waistband and a musket slung over her shoulder. Unlike me, she had another rifle in her hand. But arrows don't care how many guns you have.

"Knowing Hans, he's probably wanting to ride today," I said, wishing one of my hands was free to hold a gun. "And if he's not, he will be when he finds out what Jenkins did."

"I hope we catch them," she said, her words stinging with anger.

"We?" I asked. "No, there is no we. If Hans wants to go after them, he and I will go alone, and you'll stay with the Hastings family."

"Pa has only one good leg and arm. What good will he be to you if you do catch them?" She sat up a little taller in the saddle. "No; you need me. I'm a better shot than either of you. Pa knows."

"You may be a better shot, but you are also with my child, and I won't risk either of you getting hurt. I shouldn't have let you come with me." I shook my head. "Promises."

She smiled.

We rounded a curve and started up a small hill. Both of us reined our horses to a stop and shouldered our rifles. On top of the hill was an Indian on a horse.

He had both hands raised, palms out. "Je viens en paix!" His voice was deep and assertive.

Lotte touched my arm, lowering my rifle. "He says he comes in peace."

The red man's horse moved, and he dropped a hand to hold him. In doing so, the Indian turned his head. The scar on the side of his face was exposed between the lines of the white and red paint.

I glanced at her. "It's the same man who saved us. How do you know what he's saying?"

"All Dutch learn at least French and German," she said, slinging her musket over her saddle pommel. "He's speaking French."

"He's wearing war paint and has obviously sided with the French." I started to raise my gun again, and she stopped me.

"Most of the Indians in this part of the British America speak French as a common language," she said. "They were taught by the French monks decades ago."

"Ask him what tribe he belongs to," I asked.

"Tu es de quille tribu?" Lotte yelled.

"Lenape," he replied as a breeze fluttered the feathers intertwined in his long, braided hair.

"That's a local tribe who've sided with the French," I said, flexing my jaw muscles and never taking my eyes off the Indian. "I don't think we can trust him."

"He saved our lives just a few weeks ago."

I risked a glance at her. Those wide blue eyes were fixed on me.

"Ask him his name?"

"Votre nom?" she translated.

"Papunuck," he said and touched his chest.

"Nous sommes Hamish et Lotte." Lotte said, first pointing at me and then her.

Lotte and Papunuck conversed some more until Lotte seemed a bit agitated.

"What?" I asked. "What is he saying?" I started to lift my rifle.

"No Hamish." Lotte glanced away half-smiling. "He said he's watched, ah, me for a long time. He thinks I'm a fine woman who works hard, is a great hunter, and is worth many ponies." Her eyes returned to me. "But he's not sure about you. You shoot too many guns." Her lip quirked as she eyed my edgy, musket-holding arm.

I relaxed my grip on the weapon. "He didn't say that."

"Oh, but he did. But you did not shoot at him. And I told him that."

I huffed. Of course not, he'd saved Lotte and now I knew why. I'd have to keep an eye on him.

I rubbed my chin, if he'd been watching us, I wondered what else he'd seen. "Ask him if he saw six white men on this trail today?"

She spoke loud, strange-sounding words up the hill on which the red man sat majestically on his mount.

His responding words, though foreign to Hamish, resounded with contempt as he pointed to the trail beyond him.

"Yes, they rode north toward the white mines," Lotte said.

"Tell him we are chasing them," I said, straining to control my normally docile Rosey as she snorted and impatiently fidgeted. I was having trouble controlling her as well as the packhorse with one hand. But I couldn't sling my musket; not yet. "They robbed us. Can he take us to them?"

After another exchange, Lotte said, "He will take us. No Indians will hurt us if we are with him."

I looked at Lotte and slung my rifle. "What choice do we have? Tell him we thank him and will follow him."

But my shoulder muscles didn't relax, nor did I stop sweating.

Papunuck, on his painted pony, led us over the tree-lined trail as if the three of us were on a Sunday ride in the Scottish country side.

To my chagrin, Lotte had cross-slung her rifles over her shoulders.

At this rate, we would either catch Jenkins or be at the Hastings place way before sunset.

In a valley in the trail where a burbling creek had to be crossed, the Indian stopped and pointed into the trees on his right on the opposing watershed across the flow.

As we rode up to him, I saw fresh blood splattered on the foliage on both sides of the trail. Then the smell engulfed me; the putrid, eye-watering, clinging odor of death.

Lotte, a hand holding a handkerchief over her nose, and I, unfortunately with both hands busy, reined in our horses next to him. I looked where he pointed. Several paces off the trail, tied to stout saplings were what was left of the mangled, naked bodies of three men. My stomach contracted.

Thwarting regurgitation, I shouted, "Lotte, don't look." I was too late. She was gasping, her head turned toward the butchery.

Lotte quickly turned her head away from the gore. Her closed-eyed grimace expressing both shock and fear. She opened her eyes, fixed on me. "Who . . . who are they?" Her voice cracked.

I could hardly stomach another look, but I forced myself. The bodies had their abdomens hacked open and their intestines tied to young trees. Obviously they had been forced to walk around the saplings, disemboweling themselves until they either passed out or died.

Dozens of buzzards, crows, and wild hogs were contesting for a meal, and quite a bit had already been consumed.

It was hard to identify them with their scalps missing and their faces streaked with blood. However, what was left of the face of one of the men, though frozen in horror, was familiar. He was one of the miners; ironically, the one who feared hanging.

"They're Jenkins' men," I said softly with my head turned away, staring at Papunuck.

"Papunuck, did . . . did your people do this?" she asked, without looking at him.

"Yes. The warriors of my tribe did this. And they would do the same to you if I were not with you."

Lotte dropped her reins and grabbed my arm as a shudder coursed through her.

I clamped her hand.

My eyes returned to Papunuck's void-of-emotions stare. How could I trust a man who was not affected by this inhuman slaughter? A man whose people could do such horrible things to other human beings?

Then I remembered the staked Indians bodies lining the entrance to the stockade at Reading.

I involuntarily shook my head. Hate ruled this world I had escaped to.

Was Papunuck leading us to our own hideous death?

If he was, I'd make sure I killed him first.

If he wasn't, not only had the Indians slowed down Jenkins, they had increased the odds for me to go after the money alone.

Papunuck's words echoed in my head. Lotte and I had no choice. Without this red man, we'd soon face a horrible death. He was our only chance for survival.

Lotte unslung one of her guns from her shoulder. We rode on through the fear.

Miles later, we halted upon a wooded ridge overlooking the Hastings' farm.

This was the first time I had gotten close to the man in untainted air. His skin had a shine to it, like it was coated with something. I expected to smell the unpleasant odor of a soiled body. I was surprised. He smelled different, an oil like smell. I guess he had rubbed some animal's fat on his skin.

Papunuck, in the cover of the trees, pointed at the house. "Les homes sont là-bas."

"Their trail leads there," Lotte told me. "Are the Hastings involved in this robbery?"

I mulled over what she had asked. "I don't think so. They seem like fine people to me. We traveled together from Philadelphia to Lancaster. I think Jenkins is just reporting in as he promised to his boss. That way he can leave tomorrow with no one suspecting anything."

"I pray you're right for Pa's sake."

"We need to get down there. Thank Papunuck and ask him if there is anything we can do for him?"

Lotte translated.

Panunuck eyed my pack saddle and spoke.

"He would like one of your rifles," Lotte said.

I glanced at him and then looked away. I was being squeezed between indebtedness and treason. These were long rifles. They could kill at over three-hundred yards. How many white people would he kill with our gun?

Papunuck had saved our lives twice now. Would one rifle make a difference in this war? Probably not, though it could cost more lives.

I turned to Lotte. "Tell him on one condition, this rifle will be used only for hunting game, not killing white people," I said, as I pulled the pack horse up next to me.

Papunuck absorbed Lotte's words as he glared at me. A long moment filled with tension passed. Then he nodded.

I retrieved a musket, a bag of balls, wadding, and a powder horn and handed them to the Indian.

He weighted the rifle in his hands, then looked at me. "Me watch Hamish; shoot long," he said, surprisingly in English.

Then he smiled and rode off.

Chapter Fifty-Five

There wasn't much daylight left when Lotte and I approached what was left of the Hastings' farm. My head swiveled from side to side looking for any trace of Jenkins and his men. I saw none, except for several horse tracks coming and leaving.

George came out of the barn, rifle in hand. "Hamish," his eyes scanned Lotte, "how'd you two get here? Jenkins was just here. The Indians attacked them, taking three of his men on their way home. I should've never let him or you go."

"You were right . . . at least about Jenkins and his men," I said, dismounting. "How long have you known him?"

"Only since we came here. As long as you've known Hans. Jenkins worked for my dad probably a year before I arrived. Dad thought he was great. He's a hard worker and a good foreman. He and his men are very productive. Why are you asking about Jenkins?"

"So the mine does well?" I asked, helping Lotte off her horse. "Better than farming?"

"Dad was a wise man. We are doing very well thanks to all the gun and wagon manufacturing in the area. If it wasn't for this damned war, we'd be very happy. Why all of the questions?"

"George, this is Hans's daughter, Lotte," I said, not bothering to answer him. I helped Lotte off her horse.

"How *did* you two get here?" George asked again.

"We got through because——"

"Because we were lucky," Lotte said, saving me a long complicated explanation.

"I'd say," George said. "Joshua," he called over his shoulder.

The young man came out of the barn.

"Water and feed their horses," George said. He turned to us. "Hans will be glad to see you two. We almost had to tie him up to keep him from going home by himself today."

Lotte and I exchanged a glance.

Joshua trotted out of the barn and took the reins to our horses.

"Joshua," I addressed the young man, "for the time being leave my horse here and saddled."

"What's going on, Hamish?" George asked.

"Do you trust Mister Jenkins?" Lotte asked.

"Sure . . . yes, I do."

"Do you trust him to deliver the ore to Lancaster and Philadelphia and come back with the money?" I asked.

"Well . . . no. Dad and Mom used to do that before the Indian attacks started. Of late, Joshua and I along with a couple of the men take the ore. The men never see the money. Dad said we should never tempt them."

Lotte and I slapped the dust off our clothes and went into the barn.

Hans was standing on one leg by a cot. He shook his head. "Are you crazy!" His eyes went past me to Lotte, whom he limped to and wrapped in his arms. "Thank God you got here unscathed."

"This was my idea, Pa," Lotte said, breaking his bear-hug. "Hamish didn't want to bring me. I left him no choice."

I faced George. "How long ago did Jenkins leave?"

"Not long, not long at all. Less than an hour." He turned to Martha for confirmation. "Why didn't the two of you come with them?"

I glanced at Hans. "Because we're chasing them."

"Chasing Jenkins? I don't understand," George said.

"Unfortunately, we tempted them," I said.

"What are you talking about, Hamish?" Hans asked.

"Jenkins and his men couldn't help but see all the money I collected from selling our guns yesterday. They robbed us this morning; two-hundred-forty-six pounds."

Everyone in the room gasped.

"That's a fortune," Martha said.

"You did not collect that much money yesterday," Hans said.

"No," I said, the word dripping with shame. "It was either give them everything you had in your chest or they were going to—"I lowered my head—"Lotte."

"Get my over-under, Hamish, and saddle my horse," Hans ordered. "Those scoundrels will wish the Indians had finished them after I am done with them."

"I can't believe Jenkins would do that," George said shaking his head. "He's proved his trust many times over, though we've never tested him with large sums of money."

"He and his men had never seen the quantity of money I collected from you and the other farmers yesterday," I said. "He told me as much. It changed them."

"I will kill them; all of them!" Hans grabbed his jacket off the post.

"I'll go with you," George said. "They were going home. I feel responsible. I'll show you where they live." He turned to his son. "Joshua, saddle Hans's and my horses. Then I want you to stay here with the women."

I watched Hans almost fall as he limped out of the barn. I wanted to ask him if he was capable of riding, but I already knew the futility in asking.

The light was fading when we got to the cluster of cabins where the miners lived. Light streamed from the windows of all the cabins.

Fortunately for Hans, the trip was short, less than a mile. He had softly grunted and groaned most of the way; constantly shifting in the saddle.

George and I dismounted, and I helped Hans off his mount.

I peered through the trees as George tied the horses to an elm. "They never thought Lotte and I would follow them. They probably packed those wagons sitting between the cabins when they got home. They'll leave at first light."

"Do you know which cabins the three are in?" Hans asked.

"Yes, it's Carl Perkins and Stanislav Borsik," George said. "They too I trusted." He sighed. "They live on each side of Jenkins, and that's his cabin to the left of the wagons. Do you have a plan?"

"Well, since I am not in the best of shape, I will stay here." Hans had placed the double barrels of his rifle in the fork of a tree on the edge of the woods. The butt of his weapon rested on his lap as he leaned against an adjacent tree. "You go knock on the right cabin door and take that man as quietly as you can. I will cover the other two cabins with this double barrel; in case they hear you and try to run. I hope they try to escape." He primed his gun. "If the other two don't hear you, then you can go get Jenkins, followed by the third."

"You don't have much light left," I said.

"I have enough," Hans said.

"Soon all you'll be able to see is figures. Don't be shooting George or me."

"Surely you trust me by now, lad," Hans said and slapped my calf.

"They normally have a couple of men patrolling in case the Indians attack," George said. "With what Jenkins and his men have been through today, they won't be on guard duty. I'll make sure they see me and then there shouldn't be a problem." He stepped into the clearing and waved at a man at one end of the cabins. The man waved back. Then he did the same with a second man at the other end.

George motioned to me and we ran through the dim light to the first cabin. We leaned against the logs, listening; soft voices of a man and woman.

"You stay on one side of the door, I'll knock," I whispered and cocked my pistol. "If he asks who it is, you tell him it's Jenkins. When he opens the door I'll stick this gun in his face. You stay put in case he someway surprises me. He'll be nervous."

I stood on the opposite side of the door from the leather hinges and softly knocked.

"Who is it?" a male voiced called.

I motioned to George.

"Jenkins," he whispered in a deep voice.

The door opened inward splashing the ground with light. I jumped into the opening with my gun pointed into the room.

A big-eyed man dressed in a nightshirt, jerked backwards. Aiming the weapon at his chest, I pressed a finger to my lips. When I stepped into the cabin George followed. We tied both the man and woman up and gagged them.

"You stay here," I whispered to George. "I want to be the one who captures Jenkins."

"If you try the same approach, Jenkins will know it's you because of your brogue," George said.

"I'll say I'm Borsik. He also has an accent."

"I'll go with you," George said.

We scurried the forty or fifty yards to the next cabin. I stood next to the door until my breathing returned to normal.

I knocked lightly.

"Who's there?" Jenkins deep voiced resounded.

"Perkins," George said softly.

The door opened, and I bolted into the light with my gun pointed. A woman, standing against the far wall of the room, screamed. Then the door slammed into me hard, knocking me down and causing my pistol to discharge.

Jenkins kicked the door closed and was on me like a hungry wolf. He picked me up off the floor like I was a child.

Just as George opened the door, Jenkins hit me knocking me into George, tumbling both of us out the door into the semi-darkness.

A gun boomed from the woods chipping the logs of the cabin just over my head. I scampered on all fours to a nearby tree.

Hans's words echoed in my head, "Surely you trust me by now, lad."

"Hans, it's me!" I yelled across the clearing.

The lights in the cabin were extinguished.

George was no where in sight.

I pulled the second pistol from my jacket pocket and crawled to a nearby tree. Sitting against the elm, I primed my weapon and watched the opening to Jenkins' cabin. I slowing opened, wiggled, and closed my jaw. Though sore, nothing seemed to be broke. I cocked the gun.

The woman was pushed out.

She was crying hysterically.

Thank God Hans didn't shoot.

Then a shadow of a man, which had to be Jenkins, slithered out like a snake on his belly and wiggled his way around the corner of the house. He moved so fast, I didn't have time to take an accurate shot. He had dragged something that made clinking noises; the money bag.

I slid onto my belly and crawled after him.

It was a moonless night. I couldn't see anything. If I couldn't see him, he couldn't see me. After I slinked passed the wagon, I jumped to my feet.

Reins slapped meat and a horse galloped away.

Jenkins was leaving with the money.

I turned. "Hans, don't shoot! it's me." I ran toward the woods and our horses.

The door to the third cabin opened. I glanced over my shoulder as a man came out with a gun. He shouldered it and aimed at me. I dove.

Hans's musket boomed again. The man fell.

I jumped up and trotted past Hans to the horses. "Thanks," I said, as I untied my mount. I checked to see if my two muskets were still strapped to my saddle and climbed on. Slinging one of the guns over my shoulder, I fisted the other.

"Wait, Hamish, I am going with you."

"I can't wait. Jenkins is getting away." I kicked the horse and galloped toward the houses.

Chapter Fifty-Six

Mounted, I trotted past George in the middle of the clearing. He stood in the middle of several of the miners who had surrounded him with lanterns.

I flashed past the wagons as I galloped into the night. It was totally black all around me; I couldn't see anything in front of me, not even my horse's head. Standing in the stirrups, I pulled back hard on the reins.

Stopped, I eased into the saddle.

Other than my mount panting, I heard nothing. Not another horse galloping, crickets, tree frogs, nothing.

Jenkins couldn't see either. He had to have stopped. He was out there in the dark waiting for me. I knew it. I drew one of my pistols and cocked it.

"Hamish, are you there?" George half-whispered behind me.

Uncocking my pistol, I turned the horse and walked him back to the lit cabins.

George hunkered behind the cabins in the dim light from a rear window of an adjacent miner's home.

"Jenkins galloped into the darkness. He had to have stopped," I whispered.

George nodded. "You're right, he stopped," he said softly, handing me my other pistol. "This was in Jenkins' cabin on the floor."

"Thank you," I said stuffing the weapon in my jacket.

"Maybe a hundred yards behind these cabins is a dense forest," George said quietly. "There's a winding wagon trail through those woods we use to take ore to Philadelphia. But it's almost impossible to find that trail on a moonless night, like tonight. And if you find it, it would be hard to stay on it. So Jeremiah Jenkins is out there, waiting for either you or light, or both."

"Do me a favor and take Hans back to your place tonight," I said. "I don't want him trying to go with me at first light.

George rubbed his chin. "Based on how he rode over here, I doubt he'll be able to get back on his horse without help."

"I know."

"What'll I tell him? He'll want to chase after you."

"Tell him I rode off into the darkness behind the cabins. He won't be able to find me. It's not a lie."

"Listen to me, at first light, you can find the trail and it's only about a half mile to a vast flat meadow. If Jenkins isn't waiting for you in the woods, you'll see him in that wide-open flat ground. My family and I will take care of Hans and Lotte until you get back. Be careful,

Jenkins isn't a stupid man. And he's a brute. Don't let him get his hands on you."

"I know," I said touching my swollen jaw.

"Good luck," George said.

Chapter Fifty-Seven

I slept propped up against the outside back wall of a cabin. Thanks to Hans, I was used to getting up before dawn. The morning was cool; fall was in the air.

I drank some water out of a creek and watered my horse.

Armed with a pistol in my coat and two shoulder cross-slung muskets, I mounted my horse. I had the second pistol cocked and in my free hand.

At first light I was mounted and on the move, walking my horse to the edge of the woods behind the cabins. Though the visibility was poor, my head swiveled back and forth looking for any movement.

Eyes were on me, I knew it.

Realizing how rigid I had become, I reined in my horse and took several deep breaths. The chilled morning air cleared my mind. Then George's words from last night returned. 'Jenkins isn't a stupid man.'

I studied the woods until my eyes finally found the entrance to the trail. Just as I turned into the trail, I heard a faint slap followed by a horse clopping quite a distance in front of me. I nudged my mount and rode into the darkness.

I thought about what I'd do if I were Jenkins. At first light I would've been in the woods watching the clearing behind the cabins to see if someone was pursuing me.

I stopped my horse.

My senses were right. Jenkins had to have been watching me.

I turned my mount and rode out of the woods, turning away from the opening.

Deep inside the woods on the trail, it would have been easy for Jenkins to see me in the ring of light at the opening to the path.

I was there; I was him.

In the dark, he had waited for me to enter the trail.

Then he'd dismounted and slapped his horse to make it walk away, making me think he was getting away.

He was hiding just ahead in the shadows off the trail with a cocked musket, one of Hans' and my muskets . . . and all of our money.

Jaws clenched, I dismounted and tied my horse to a tree. I looked up. The sky was now gray versus black. It would soon be daylight.

As soon as he realized my horse and I were no longer on the trail, he'd make a run for the flatlands; or at least that's what I'd do if I were him.

I had to find him before he did that.

Both pistols drawn, primed, and cocked, I crouched down and scampered into the trees.

Trying to be as quiet as possible, I made my way through the dense, dew-dripping woods and undergrowth.

Fifty or sixty paces in, I was soaked from the waist down. But I had been quiet.

Then I heard tree limbs swishing and snapping. Jenkins had discovered I wasn't riding into the tunnel anymore. He was fleeing.

I turned and bolted toward where I'd tied my horse. Halfway there I heard a horse neigh behind me and hoofs clopping into a gallop.

My wet legs hopped and weaved at an out-of-control speed. I couldn't let him get away. Hans and I had worked too hard.

I was on my horse, recklessly galloping through the dim, winding, knobby trail.

I leaned close to her ear and whispered, "We can do this, Rosey. Come on, girl."

If this were another one of Jenkins tricks, I was in trouble. I did have a few things in my favor; the light was bad; and I was low in the saddle and moving very fast over the twisting and turning path.

Leaning with my mount, we rounded a tight curve and there in my view was the end of the woods. There was no sign of Jenkins in the flatlands beyond the woods.

I kicked my horse pushing her to her limits.

Just as we exploded out of the forest, so did a seemingly distant rifle. Shockingly I felt nothing and my horse seemed unaffected. I glanced left, nothing; right and there maybe a hundred yards away was an Indian with a smoking rifle braced on a log.

I stood in the saddle and slowed my steed. When stopped I turned my mount.

There by the trail opening from the woods was a big man on the ground and a musket nearby. A horse was tied to a log behind him.

Jenkins' horse.

I looked back at the Indian as he mounted his pony. He raised the rifle over his head. A gust of wind blew his long hair away from his scarred cheek.

Chapter Fifty-Eight

With the sun still blocked by the eastern trees, I sat on Rosey and watched Papunuck disappear into the woods.

Papunuck had broken his promise.

He had used our long rifle to shoot a white person; Jenkins.

Thank God.

Once again, he'd saved my life. I wondered if I would ever be able to repay him.

I rode back to the fallen Jenkins. Dismounting, I took a few steps to check if he were still alive, but stopped; a chunk of his head was missing. I closed my eyes quickly and turned away.

I would have felt sorry for Jenkins except he was about to kill me.

My red friend could shoot; a head shot from at least two-hundred yards.

I went to Jenkins' horse and found the money bag. It had to weigh at least four stones. Had he kept all the money to himself? Clearing a spot on the ground, I dumped the contents and counted it. All two-hundred-forty-six pounds were there.

Mid-morning, with Jenkins's body flopped over his saddle and the heavy money bag slung over mine, I returned to the Hastings farm.

I dismounted and tied the horses to a tree.

Hastings, Hans, and Lotte greeted me at the barn entrance.

Hans looked over my shoulder at the tied horses. "So you killed the bastard, Hamish." He slapped me on the shoulder. "Good man."

I slid the bag off my sagging shoulder and set it on the dirt at his feet.

"What's that?" he asked, looking from the bag to me.

"Your money."

"My money, did you get all of it?" He bent to grab it and a groan escaped his mouth.

I stopped him. "It's heavy. Don't lift it. It's all there. Obviously Jenkins wasn't planning on sharing his loot with his few remaining partners." I sat the bag next to Lotte's bedroll and musket.

"He was not a good man, but you *are*." Hans wrapped his unwounded ape like arm around my back and squeezed me.

"Thank God you're back," Lotte said with a beaming smile and touched my hand.

Just her slight touch sent a surge of warmth through me on this cool morning.

"I second that comment, Hamish," George said. "It was taking all of our efforts to keep Hans from going after you."

"Let the boy come in," Martha said standing behind them. "He looks like he could use a cup of my hot tea."

"Joshua," George said, "go take care of the horses and—"

"No," I inserted. "That is my mess to clean up. I will take care of it."

Palms up, George nodded.

Clean from my challenging chores, I was sitting at a makeshift table in the barn, sipping tea. George and his mother, Rebecca, his wife, Martha, and his son, Joshua, along with Hans and Lotte had joined me. For the first time in the past week, all of my kinked tension was gone.

"So tell us what happened?" Martha asked.

My shoulders and neck again tightened. I should've known she would ask the question I didn't want to answer.

I glanced at Lotte. If I recounted everything that happened, she would probably be the only one that would accept the truth; there are good Indians.

I took my time finishing my tea, collecting my thoughts. I had been hiding so many truths, this was not the time to hide more.

"I didn't kill Jenkins."

"What?" Hans sat more upright.

"I'm not sure I would have if given the opportunity. I just wanted to get our money back and capture him. Let other men be the judge of his transgressions."

"But that was him with a chunk of his head missing over his saddle was it not?" George asked.

"Yes."

"Then who killed him?" Martha again.

I folded my arms across my chest. "A Lenape Indian named Papunuck."

All of them gasped except Lotte, she smiled.

"The same red man who spared Lotte's and my lives when she stepped into the bear trap in the woods a month or so ago." I glanced at each of them. "The same *savage* who escorted Lotte and I up the miner's trail yesterday on which minutes earlier three of Jenkins men were slaughtered by people from Papunuck's tribe. And just a bit ago, the Indian who shot Jenkins just as he was going to ambush me; probably kill me."

This time Lotte gasped.

I looked at Hans. "Papunuck head-shot Jenkins from over two-hundred yards."

"That's some shot," Hans said.

"He did it with one of our new muskets," I said sitting up taller.

Hans stood, disregarding his bad leg and shaking his head. "He has one of our new guns? How did he get that?"

"I gave it to him for bringing Lotte and I here safely."

"He is an Indian, a killer of white people," Hans said as if each word tasted foul.

I unfolded my arms. "Papunuck is Lotte's and my friend."

"Yes, he is," Lotte said, her pale eyes fixed on mine.

Hans eased into his chair.

"I was always told there is no such thing as a good Indian," Joshua said.

An unsettling quiet filled the room.

Rebecca stood. "When your grandfather and I first came here, the Indians were good to us, including the Lenapes. Many were actually our friends as well." Her features changed from complacent to stern. "Least ways until things went bad between the British and French. Since then, we haven't been very good to our red friends."

To my surprise, Hans sighed and nodded.

The truth relieved me. I glanced from Lotte to Hans. Soon, God-willing, I would have no secrets.

Chapter Fifty-Nine

"I've got to hire more miners, plus take Perkins to the fort for trial," George said, standing in the barn door with the sun almost directly overhead. "We talked it over this morning," he motioned to the two women, "and we'd like to come with you to Lancaster. We'll need to pack up a few things; take maybe an hour. We'll probably be there a week or two."

"That's kind of you," I said. "We could use the numbers."

"I sent Joshua to get a couple of the miners and their families to stay here while we're gone. Hopefully they'll keep the Indians from burning the rest of it." George looked around the property as he hitched horses to a wagon.

The effect the tree-covered wagon trail to Lancaster had on me hadn't changed. My neck hairs bristled, and sweat ran down the valley in my back despite the cool early fall air.

On horseback, I led, pistol in hand, followed by Lotte cradling her musket.

Hans, Martha, Rebecca, and Perkins' wife rode in a carriage along with Hans' hefty money bag.

Last came George and Joshua on a wagon stuffed with supplies and a tied up Perkins. Joshua was turned to watch our rear.

Each carried their new Blekkink long rifle.

Han's horse along with George's horse were tied to the rear of the coach.

With the sun touching the western treetops, we arrived at Hans' home.

We hadn't seen an Indian. Maybe Papunuck was still watching over us.

Lotte dismounted.

"George, you and your family can stay with us," Hans said, as he slowly climbed down from the carriage. "We have extra rooms. After all you've done for me, I would be pleased if you accepted."

"Thank you, Hans, but we are the ones indebted to you for saving us and taking two arrows in the process." He shook Hans' offered hand. "We need to deliver Perkins to the authorities. And besides, we want to be in town, where the workers are. We'll stay at the fort tonight. and make other arrangements with friends in town tomorrow."

Joshua untied Hans' horse and handed me the reins. "You are the bravest man I've ever known," he said, looking up at me on my horse. Then he turned and walked away.

He nodded at me and climbed on the wagon replacing his dad who now drove the carriage. Their little caravan drove away.

Lotte unlocked the house and went inside.

I took the horses to the barn.

"I have been wanting to talk with you, Hamish, just you and I," Hans said from behind me.

I dismounted. As I opened the barn door, I noticed my hands were shaking. It was time. I dreaded what was about to take place, but it had to happen. Hans needed to know everything.

Chapter Sixty

It was the end of a cool October day when the light was golden and the quiet loud.

Hans hobbled into the barn, as I unsaddled Rosey. She and I both needed a bath after the long day of travel to the Hastings yesterday, chasing Jenkins all morning, and then coming home.

He leaned against the side of the stall. "When we were in the woods outside the Hastings' farm and you were about to remove that arrow from my leg, did you say you were in love with Lotte? Did I hear you correctly?"

I heaved the wooden saddle on top of the stall wall. Then I turned and looked Hans in the eyes. It was hard for me to think of him as Lotte's father; he was my friend, my best friend.

I briefly glanced away as I thought about how much I loved his daughter. Then I slowly nodded as our eyes met again. "Yes, I love your daughter more than *anything* in this world."

His forehead creased. "Does she know how you feel?"

"Yes," I answered wishing I had something to do with my hands. So I began brushing Rosey, as she whinnied and her coat shimmied in response.

"And does she love you as well?"

"Yes, but you should ask her."

"I trust you, Hamish." He pushed upright off the wall.

There was that trust word again; a knife to my conscience.

Hans' face crinkled into a smile. "I must say I am happy about this. I have often thought of you as a son."

I wanted to be his son. More than anything, I wanted to be a part of this family. But my joyous reaction was drowning in guilt.

"You are a good lad, Hamish. Do you think your love for Lotte and hers for you is strong enough to last at least four years? Lotte will be leaving soon for the Amsterdam, thank God. She'll be away from this horrible place."

"I know, sir, and I—"

"Now, now, son, don't worry. I plan on keeping you very busy for the next four years. Thanks to you, we've made a weapon so fine everyone wants one. I think between the two of us we can figure out how to make it for less cost and maybe even improve it."

"We can do that, sir, but I—"

"Let me finish, son. While you've been falling in love with my daughter, I have been thinking about our future; yours and mine. I want to shorten your indenture term from seven years to two. You have more than earned that. And then, if all goes well next year, I want to make you a partner where we will share the costs and the profits. How does that sound?" He slapped me on the shoulder.

I looked away at nothing, I couldn't breathe, I was reeling as if I were in a mid-Atlantic storm again. I half-stumbled as I left the stall and walked over to Hans's horse and removed the heavy bag of money Joshua had thrown over the saddle. I dropped the bundle of coins on the straw-covered ground.

Hans limped over to me. He spread his hands. "Don't you have anything to say? I thought my offer would have made you extremely happy?"

I worked on removing the saddle as if he weren't there. I didn't know where to begin. I didn't want to hurt him, but I knew I had to tell him everything. I plopped the saddle on top of the stall wall next to the one I'd just removed from Rosey. Then I stopped, unmoving, too many thoughts booming in my head.

"Hamish, what is wrong?" Hans asked, with a tone of disbelief.

I slowly turned and faced him. He had sat down on a stool just beyond the stall.

"Hans, your reaction . . . your offer——,"shaking my head, I blew out a held breath——"you don't really know me. I, I came here because I killed a young boy in Scotland." Again I could envision the small lad's cold eyes. The old familiar ache in my gut came to life.

"What?" Hans asked with a lined forehead.

I sighed. "His older brute of a brother was trying to rob me and threatening me with a knife. My family depended on that money for food. I flung a brick at him and he ducked and . . . and I killed his little brother. He was only a . . . a child."

Hans' frown lessened. "Hamish, what a terrible thing to have happened. But it sounds like self-defense to me; like an accident."

"It would have been my word against Bruce's. And If I were found innocent, Bruce would have killed me sooner or later. I had to leave."

"You are not a killer, Hamish. I remember how upset you were about killing those Indians who tried to get into our home."

I looked away.

Hans slapped his good leg. "Hamish, I *do* know you. And I know you would never kill a person unless a loved-one was threatened. I know you carry the guilt of all you have seen here, even the deaths you have had nothing to do with. You are a good man. Hamish. A man I know. A man I trust."

His words caused me to bow my head for a moment. Then, straightening, I looked the stout, father-like man in his pale blue eyes. "You don't know me, sir. I violated your trust."

"And how did you do that?" he said with his head tilted and one eyebrow raised.

Holding his inquisitive eyes, I softly said, "Lotte's with child."

Chapter Sixty- One

The weight of my words drooped Hans' shoulders. His mouth hung open almost touching his chest as he hunkered on the stool and stared at the straw at his feet.

A long moment passed with neither of us moving.

The light was fading and shadows grew out of the barn floor.

Finally, Hans braced his arms on his legs and straightened. His expression though now blank was given away by his cold eyes fixed on mine. "You *are* right. I do not know you." His deep voice flat, yet chilling.

I simply stood there, slathered in guilt and defenseless against his battering words. Though wishing he hadn't agreed with me, I didn't have a reply.

Hans struggled to his feet, a roar bursting from deep within him, and flung the stool into the barn wall shattering the three-legged chair.

I flinched and gritted my teeth. Both shock and fear slammed me. I had never seen this side of Hans. Summoning all my courage, I stood my ground against his anger.

He pointed at the broken remnants. "Shattering that stool is what you have done to Lotte's dream, her gifted future, her chance to further her education, her safety." His voice dropping from a shout to a whisper. "All you young men think about is your moment of pleasure. You never consider the consequences until it is too late."

"But—"

"But nothing! Did you ever think of *her*? Giving birth to a child could kill her!" He spread his arms, hands fisted.

"God-forbid something bad happens to Lotte." Chin falling, I staggered a step back. My stomach was trying to eat its way out of me. I hadn't thought about . . . I hadn't thought. My guilt multiplied tenfold.

"Do you have any idea of what people will say to her when as an unwed mother she starts showing? And if she and the baby survive, do you have any idea of the shame she would face every day . . . that we'd both face?" He dropped his arms. "No. No, you never thought of that either."

"I love her." I raised my bowed head. "Although I wish I could, I cannot undo what has happened." I squared my shoulders. "I want to marry her and father our child. Please let me do what is the right thing for all of us."

He limped-paced back and forth in front of me. Then he stopped and pointed at me. "Do not tell me *now* what is right. If you had done the right thing when I left, entrusting you with the care of my daughter, you would never have impregnated her." Hans made the most wonderful moment in my life sound cheap, wrong.

Dropping his pointing hand, Hans eased his weight off his wounded leg by leaning against a stall. "I moved you into my room from the shop . . . my room. I should have put you in the barn and left you there. Neither you nor this problem you have created would be here now; not after the Indian attack."

The man I respected for his physical strength and inventive mind, now seemed weak and lost. He looked down, shaking his head. "I made a big mistake. I thought after all the time you and I had spent together that I knew you; that I could trust you. I thought you and I had become close; family close like a father and son." He took a deep breath and eased it out as he shut his eyes. "I, I loved you." His voice had become soft and frail, weakened by pain. His eyelids raised revealing two dull, lifeless orbs. "As I said, I made a big mistake."

"Hans, I—"

His head snapped up as he shoved his open palm at me. "I . . . I thought we had a great deal in common. I thought we were both decent, caring men. Men who respected others and their property." He grimaced and looked away. "I was wrong."

Hans again limped back and forth in front of me, hands clenched behind his back. "Lotte and I have told you everything about us."

He stopped. "You . . . you have secrets."

Hans limped on.

He stopped, his eyes void of emotions. "I gave you my home and my trust. And you, you took. You violated Lotte and my trust; ruining our lives."

He looked away. "You, an indentured servant, are not ready to be a father. What fool would want to bring a child into this God-forsaken world? I will tell you, a fool who is not responsible for his actions, that's who.""

His words ripped into me, making it hard to speak, but I had to for Lotte's sake. "Give us a chance. We'll get married, and she'll have the child. Then she can go to Amsterdam and pursue her dream. And after I save some money, as need be, the child and I will join her there."

"Have you listened to anything I have said? One, birthing a child could kill her. Two, a mother will never leave her child and if she did, a child should not be made to exist in this place. Three, if she did go, who would take care of the baby, nurse it, change it, doctor it, an irresponsible person like you?"

"We love each other," I said as firmly as I dare. "We just want a chance."

"You, a servant, will not tell *me* what you want. You have no more chances with my daughter. None."

"She loves me." My voice sounded thin, beaten down.

His pale but fierce eyes drilled into mine. "She will still love me long after you are gone."

He hesitated and released a small, sarcastic chuckle. "I thought you to be smart. How will you save money or go to Amsterdam with a child? You have more than six years of servitude to complete."

I bit my lower lip. He wasn't going to listen to anything I said. And I was tired of his painful replies. But I was not beaten; not yet anyway. I lifted my chin and straightened my shoulders. "So what do you want us to do?"

"Us?" he scowled. "This isn't about *us*. It is about my daughter, my only child."

He shook his head. "As for you . . . let me take an moment to think about you, the irresponsible indentured servant."

I released a breath and fought to maintain control.

Long, agonizing minutes passed.

"This is not normally done until the end of the indenture servitude term, but because of the work we have accomplished, I will very generously give you fifty pounds, a saddle and Rosey, and one of our muskets. And *you* will immediately leave here. I will pack your things and leave them on the road. You can pick them up before sunrise tomorrow on your way out of Lancaster Town."

"You are going to send me away? Away from Lotte and my child? How——"

"Away!" he boomed. "Away from *my* child." He again pointed at me, his finger shaking with anger. "Do not try to talk to my daughter, ever again. If you do, I will beat you into the dirt. Do you understand me?"

Each of his words slammed into my gut like one of his iron fists, over and over again. I wanted to vomit. For the first time in my life, I wanted to cry. All I could do was nod.

Lotte and I were done.

I would never see my child.

This couldn't be.

But his eyes told me otherwise.

I wanted to hate him, but he was right. I had violated his trust with the person he loved more than his own life.

Leaving my Scottish family behind, I had come to this country with nothing but hope and not much of that. I had contracted to be someone's slave for seven years.

Then I met the Blekkinks.

Hans whom I grew to love like a father had done nothing but give me a family that I sorely yearned for, a home, and a promising future. But more than anything, he and Lotte had given me love. I had more than I ever dreamed I would have. And now that was all gone, gone because of my mistake.

I had sullied it.

I had failed him as well as Lotte.

I had failed myself.

Overwhelmed, I turned away so he wouldn't see my tears and started saddling Rosey.

I could hear him counting out the money while I worked.

I didn't want his money. I wanted everything I was losing; his daughter, my child, his love, his home, our home.

Oddly, an old memory resurrected. When my siblings and I were children, after my father had left us, our mother would read us bedtime-stories from the Bible.

The clinking money reminded me of how Judas must have felt after betraying his master.

Chapter Sixty-Two

As darkness settled across this bloodied-land, I rode Rosey under the lamp-post, spotted lights of Lancaster Town.

Hans had cast me out.

I was hollow inside and numb outside. I wasn't sure where I was going and really didn't care.

The only things I was certain of were I couldn't return to Hans' house or stay in Lancaster Town very long.

In his finality, Hans had been stern but generous. I had the saddled-mare, the clothing on my back, a musket, a powder horn, and two bags; one filled with balls and wadding, the other with fifty pounds of coins. And tomorrow, he would place the rest of my belongings on the dirt path in front of what used to be my home.

I needed to think. A wanderer in this evil land wouldn't last long.

Then a thought struck me. I was no longer indentured. I was free to go wherever and do whatever.

My papers from ol' man MacDonald certifying that I was a Journeymen gunsmith were in the chest Hans has sent me.

Word was most of the British America was different than this western area. The eastern coastal cities neither were surrounded by Indian-infested-wilderness nor affected by the war.

I was a very good musket maker. I was sure I could get a job in a major eastern city.

I could get away from the war and make a decent wage.

But my freedom, materials things, a job, and safety all meant nothing if I didn't have Lotte and our child in my life.

I reined in Rosey, letting my mind chase answers.

The plan grew, lifting my spirits. Tonight, I'd buy two tickets on the next stage going east, hopefully tomorrow. Then, in the morning, I'd go back to Hans', as he had requested, to get my belongings. But I'd get more than my clothing,

I'd take Lotte.

We'd run away together.

We'd go to Philadelphia or better yet New York, or Boston. We'd get married, and I'd get a job as a journeyman gunsmith. The big cities would have trained, experienced mid-wives to help Lotte and the baby through the birthing.

We'd raise our baby in the safety of a large city.

I'd work my way to a master gunsmith and eventually start my own business.

I stopped at the way station where the on-going stage coach passengers could stay and where coach tickets were sold.

"When does the next stage leave?" I asked the clerk who was preparing to close.

He grimaced and shook his head. "The coach is two days overdue. With all the recent problems, the military has been supplying a five-men escort. Frank, the scheduled driver and one of our best, has always gotten through. Sometimes he's late; but never two days." He looked down and sighed. "We fear the worst. The fort's Commandant is asking for volunteers for a search party."

Chapter Sixty-Three

Thinking I may need every penny of the money Hans had given me, I slept in the way station's stables with Rosey.

Before sun-up, I chewed on a stale piece of bread I bought from the stable hand, oddly comfortable riding Rosey.

I could see my breath in the sunless fall air. I was cold. I needed my coat.

I arrived at Hans' home in the early light of day. There in the dirt path, as promised, was the wooden chest Hans had so kindly sent to Philadelphia for me when I arrived.

If I could only go back to the Coach Inn and start over.

I wondered if given the chance to relive the past many months, if I could control myself enough not to have sex with Lotte. I doubted it. Being intimate with the woman I loved was the most wonderful experience I'd ever had. I was convinced there would never be anything in my life that would top it; nothing.

I was also convinced that moment resulted in the worst experience of my life; losing everything important in my life.

The sight of the house, knowing Lotte was just steps away in the warmth of the kitchen, added to my heart-aching regret.

I wanted to sneak in there and steal Lotte. But we had nowhere to go. I wouldn't take her back into the wilderness. We had been lucky the last time.

I dismounted and as I stooped over the chest, I noticed the key was in the lock. I knelt and opened the hinged-lid. There on top of my neatly folded and stacked clothes was a note and a folded parchment.

Squatted with the box top between me and the windows of the house, I unfolded and read the note.

My dearest Hamish,

I miss you and love you beyond measure.
In mere hours our lives have been cruelly altered.

I have never seen Pa this distraught since Ma died. He told me what happened. And despite my crying and begging, he refuses to budge.
I am never to see you again.

Pa is a good man. Before you told him of my condition, if he could, he would have given either of us the moon.

This is not your fault. You did not do this by yourself. We did this deed, willingly, together. It is our mistake.

We violated his trust. We destroyed what he had worked so hard for, his dream for me, his one and only little girl.

We hurt him deeply.

We broke him.

It makes me sad to see Pa suffer. And I am so sorry that you are the sole target of his rage.

He told me he has ordered you to leave Lancaster Town this day.

Hamish, do not leave without me.

Though Pa does not know it, I stayed up most of the night packing. I am going with you. Do not worry, I did not take very much for none of it will fit me soon. My belongings are already bagged on a saddled horse in the barn.

With the money Pa has given me for schooling, you and I can start over either in another city in the British America, or Amsterdam City, Scotland, or anywhere.

I do not care where we live as long as we live together.

As soon as Pa goes to the shop tomorrow morning, *I am leaving.*
I will meet you at the centre square at mid-day.

Love forever,

Lotte

The urge to jump up and down and shout out my joy fought for release. I would be a husband and a father. Hopefully I'd be able to contain my feelings while I could be seen from the house.

The parchment caught my eye. I unfolded it. It was my indentured servant contract with Hans which I had signed in Scotland. Hans had written a note at the bottom releasing me from the contract. He had signed and dated it.

My first reaction should have been joy since I was now a free man, but it wasn't. Unlike ol' man MacDonald, Hans had made work fun with his inventiveness. I looked forward to each workday. He challenged my creativity and my skills. I was learning as well as contributing more than just labor, much more.

I was a much better gunsmith because of Hans. And we had made the best musket ever and were constantly improving our productivity with new tools and methods. Our costs were reduced as were the hours to make a gun.

Hans' signed contract was his way of saying good-bye.

I wouldn't be able to replace the times I had with Hans.

Neither Lotte or I would be the same without Hans. Would she eventually blame me for separating her from her 'Pa'? Would I ever be happy going to work again?

And I could imagine how much we would hurt Hans by Lotte running away with me. I had experienced that loss; it was horrible.

What Lotte and I were doing was wrong; wrong for Hans and yet I prayed it was right for the baby. And I prayed what we were about to do wouldn't taint our future.

I pulled on my coat and tricorne. Closing and locking the chest, I pocketed the letter, the contract, and key. Rising, a man burdened by concern, I stood, box in hand. I tied the chest to the back of the saddle.

Astride Rosey, I studied the lit windows of the house, wondering if I were being watched. It was very hard to nudge Rosey to walk away from this place; but I had no choice. The house, the shop, the barn had all become home to me.

I turned Rosey and headed back to Lancaster Town, joy and sadness at war within me.

Within the next few hours, I had to decide where Lotte and I would go and how we would get there.

Chapter Sixty-Four

By the time I had gotten to the town center, which the townspeople called centre square, I had decided.

When Lotte joined me at mid-day, we would hide until the next stage to Philadelphia was available. We'd rest there for a day or two and then take a coach to New York. From New York, we'd go to Boston.

Starting over wasn't new to me. We could do it.

Lotte and I would begin a new life. And then after the child was born, and we were settled; we'd send for Hans.

Our lives, including the baby's, wouldn't be whole without Hans. Hopefully time would have healed his wounds by then. And we would get him out of this war zone.

Despite Hans' last hateful words to me, I loved him and knew he loved me. He was just deeply hurt.

As the Town Crier rang the center's bells, atop a high post, twelve times, announcing mid-day, my excitement mounted, overwhelming my sadness.

Lotte would be here any moment.

My mind revisited the times when we had been alone together. The closeness, the warmth, the tenderness, all came to life as if I were there again.

I hoped that her missing her dad wouldn't change those feelings. But I was the reason for her leaving, how could she not blame me for her loss?

When the flow of people passing through the town center began to blur due to my clustered mind, I bought a couple of apples from a passing vendor for pennies. I polished them with my shirt tail.

Rosey snorted a rumble of air and pawed the dirt with her hoof.

I slipped one of the apples into my pocket for Lotte.

Then I held the other in my flattened palm. Rosey's lips curled back, her coarse hair tickling my hand, as she gently nipped the apple from my palm.

"I'm so glad I got to keep you, girl. We've been to the gates of hell and back eh, you and me." I ran my hand down her glossy neck and gave her a strong pat.

I glanced to the north entrance to the center. There in the distance, I saw the top of Hans' buggy, bouncing towards me. I couldn't see the driver for all the people about. Odd, Lotte's note said she had packed her horse, not the buggy.

A wedge of concern pushed into my anticipated joy.

As the carriage came into view, Hans' eyes found mine.

The tension from our last meeting crept up my back.

As Hans reined in his horse, another horse came galloping into the center from the Philadelphia road. A young man was guiding it and another man slumped behind him.

"Help! I need help," the young man shouted as he pulled his mount to a stop between Hans and I.

I stepped forward just as the man on the back slid off into my arms. It was all I could do to keep from falling with his weight. With his head on my shoulder, the man whispered, "Hamish MacCardle".

Hans was suddenly at my side and helped me ease the injured man to the ground. Though his face was puffy and bruised, I could tell he was Frank, the coach driver.

"Get . . . get the Commander. Hur-hurry," Frank said.

A nearby soldier scurried away.

A woman walked up and gave Frank a tin of water which he gulped down.

"Frank, what happened?" Hans asked, kneeling next to him, supporting his head.

"We were about halfway to Philadelphia when a company of French Regulars and dozens of Indians stopped and surrounded us. Although we had the military escort, to fight would have been suicide. They took all of us captive."

Another lady gave Frank a hunk of bread, from which he took a huge bite.

"An officer commanded most of our captors to stay there and to stop all travelers to and from Lancaster," Frank said between chews. "Roughly twenty of them took us to their camp which was close by." He finished the bread. "Their camp was huge. There had to be over two hundred Frenchmen there along with hundreds of Indians."

Frank sat up. His eyes enlarged. "The Indians started going crazy when they saw us. They wanted us. We were all terrified. If the French hadn't taken charge, I'm sure we would have been tortured and killed. They put us in a fenced-in area and we watched them finish making these large sling things. They had at least a dozen of them."

"Catapults?" a man in the crowd asked.

"Yeah, that's what they called them. And they had at least that many cannon as well."

"What the hell they got old catapults for?" another person asked.

"They're talking about burning Lancaster Town," Frank said.

"When?" Hans asked, raising.

"Soon," Frank said. "I didn't stay around to find out. That night, I slipped away and ran for days until this young man found me."

I looked at Hans. "Where is Lotte?"

"She will not be joining you," he said firmly.

"You left her home alone?" I stood.

Hans nodded.

"How did you keep her from coming?" I asked.

"She is not coming." He averted his eyes.

"You locked her up." I ran to Rosey and leapt on her back.

"Where do you think you are going?" Hans yelled limping over to me and grabbing Rosey's reins.

"Lotte can't be left there alone. What if the French attack?"

"I will get her, you stay here," Hans said.

"No!" I jerked the reins away from him and maneuvered Rosey through the crowd.

When I cleared the crowd, I nudged Rosey into a gallop heading north. I glanced over my shoulder and Hans, in his carriage, was failing to keep up with me.

Screaming at people to get out of my way, I pulled my tricorne down close to my eyes and rode Rosey as fast as I could.

I prayed the French and Indians wouldn't attack until after dark.

Chapter Sixty-Five

I found Lotte locked in her room. Hans had tied a rope to the door handle and fastened it to the door across the hall.

Lotte stood just beyond the door. I reached out and pulled her into my arms, holding her like she was my life and without her I'd die. Her warmth stole my focus.

For a long moment we were as one.

"Come," I said when I finally eased her to arms' length. "We must make haste."

"But Pa, he went to—"

"Your father should have never locked you in your room and left you here alone. There's talk of an attack on Lancaster Town. We must go. Now."

I took her small hand, and we raced down the stairs and out to the barn.

I saddled her mare and helped her up onto her mount.

As I was tying her bundle of clothing onto the back of the saddle, the sound of a carriage came rattling into the clearing past the house.

I turned just as Hans reined his horse to a stop facing us.

He shouldered his over-under musket and aimed it at me.

Though the end of the barrel looked like a cannon aimed at my chest, my pain from his actions overwhelmed my fear.

"Nothing I say is either understood or heard by you," Hans said, his words coated with anger. "*You* are not taking my daughter with you. Now help her off that horse and get on yours before I have to do something I prefer not doing." He cocked the rifle.

"So what are you going to do?" I asked. "Keep Lotte here with you while you try to defend your home against an army?"

"Those heathens cannot be allowed to have all of these weapons and ammunition."

"I think you are the one who doesn't hear very well. Frank said this army of French and Indians have catapults and cannons. And Papunuck knows we are gun makers. And he knows how superior our guns are. They *will* come here. And they *will* blow down your doors with one cannon shot and take this fortress in a blink. Lotte cannot stay here, nor should you. You cannot even walk well."

Hans glanced down and then back at me and then Lotte.

"Pa, Hamish is trying to save us," Lotte said from atop her mount. "Please listen to him."

Hans took a deep breath and blew it out. He lowered his weapon and eased the hammer down. He fumbled the gun onto his lap. Then he covered his bowed face with his shaking hands.

My eyes burned as I watched this man's pride struggle with reality. I took a step toward him. "How about I help you move your arsenal to the fort?"

He dropped his hands and sighed. His pale blue eyes, no longer conveying anger, found me. He nodded.

"Help me down, Hamish," Lotte said. "I will help you."

"No," I said. "There is much to do. Lotte, take this." I handed her my musket. "Ride to our most western neighbor and tell them what is happening. Ask them if the men will help us move our weapons. Their families should start for the fort and pass the word along the way. Then return immediately. Hans, you ride out to the tower and tell them they must pass the word tower-to-tower that a French-Indian army is going to attack soon. I would suggest they abandoned the towers and go to the fort and see what their Commander is planning. I will stay here and harness the horses to the wagon. Then I'll move the wagon to the front door so we can load it."

"Hamish, I—"

"Go," I said. "And may God be with each of us."

Chapter Sixty-Six

Other than the chest containing my possessions wedged under the seat, the walls of the Hans' wagon were lined with the little wooden canisters of powder stacked with bags of balls and wadding.

The two men and their three boys who had returned with Lotte from down the road had helped greatly.

The October short day was only hours from ending as Hans and I along with the neighbors placed the last of our muskets on top of the British 'Brown Betsies' in the wagon. A bell rang somewhere between us and town followed by a rifle shot. A second later multiple shots came from the same direction close to Lancaster Town.

A battle had broken out.

My stomach knotted; it was starting. I, along with the other men and their boys, clamored for our weapons. I grabbed Hans' arm. "The French and Indians have attacked between us and the fort. We're cut off."

The men and their sons waved good-byes as they ran toward town where their families had gone, heading to the fort.

Hans nodded. "As I have always said, these Indians are smart warriors. They probably watched and waited until we loaded all these weapons and ammunition on the wagon for them."

"The three of us can't stay here," I said. "They'll be here soon. We need to leave now."

"Where?" Hans asked.

I helped Lotte up on her horse. "Are all those guns loaded with powder and balls, Hans?"

"Certainly, all they need is priming," he said.

"You drive the wagon, Hans," I said as I mounted Rosey. "Lotte and I will follow you. We'll race down the tower line. Hopefully, we'll be able to go around the attackers and reach the fort."

"If they are watching us now," Hans' expression voiced concern, "they will cut us off."

I pondered what he said. "Sounds as if they attacked town from our side of the city, the eastern side," I said. "We'll head for town and then cut across to the tower line on the western side. I doubt if there are any French or Indians on that side of Lancaster Town."

"But Lotte—"

"We don't have any other choice, Pa." Lotte said. "I'll be fine."

I reined Rosey in behind the wagon next to Lotte. This lovely, pregnant woman, rifle in hand, sat tall in the saddle. She had supported me, and she *was* fine.

I prayed she was right.

Chapter Sixty-Seven

Hans drove into Lancaster Town; toward the blazing roof tops and the battle. The shooting, now joined by cannon fire, seemed too close. He stopped the wagon and motioned us to come forward.

Lotte and I reined in our horses next to him.

"As we thought, they are attacking from the east. Hamish, please get Lotte to safety. Take her and ride hard down the western tower line to the fort. I am going to go help those men who helped us. I guarantee you our neighbors and their boys joined this engagement. That is what we Lancaster Town men are trained to do. They will need our guns and ammunition."

"No!" Lotte screamed.

I jumped off Rosey and handed Hans my reins. "You go with Lotte. Your leg isn't good enough for battle. I'll take the wagon to them."

Hans threw Rosey's reins back at me. "You heard me." His tone softened. "Please, for once, listen to what I am asking of you. For Lotte's sake. Now go!"

"We'll all go," Lotte said and kicked her horse past us toward the shooting.

I jumped on Rosey and galloped after her with Hans and the wagon right behind me.

Damn her.

The houses were closer to each other inside the town limits. We stopped in front of two side-by-side homes whose roofs were ablaze.

I peered around the side of one of the homes. Quite a distance behind the houses, forty or fifty men and boys had gathered behind a chest-high stone wall close to the tower line. Chunks of the barrier had been blown away by cannon shot. The ground was littered with bodies on both sides of the stone border.

Lotte and I stopped, shielded from the enemy's gunfire by a large home.

Hans whipped the horses past the house toward the fight.

"No!" Lotte screamed.

I grabbed her reins to keep her from following.

I watched Hans whip the horses through the open space, stopping close to the wall with a stone smoke house between him and the battle.

I dismounted and helped Lotte off her horse. I handed her Rosey's reins. "Tie the horses up and stay here. Please."

She nodded. "Keep him safe, Hamish."

Rifle in hand, I ran low around the house several hundred yards to Hans.

The stocky Dutchman, his back to me, was stacking our rifles against the lowered tailgate as I sprinted toward him. When he heard me running he whirled around with a cocked musket aimed from his waist.

I slid to a stop, hands raised.

His expression foretold his words. "I wasn't sure who was running at me. You, you were supposed to . . . I should have known you would not abide by my wishes." He lowered the weapon. "Is Lotte with you?"

I nodded.

"It's too late to argue," he said. He picked up one of our guns and patted it. "May our guns be as good as I dreamt them to be. Help me. We need to carry as much of this material as we can to the wall, Hamish."

Hans and I strapped our chests with powder horns and bags of shot and wadding. Then, with arms full of our guns, we raced low and as fast as Hans could hobble to the barrier.

Several of the men slapped Hans on the back.

"Fellow gunsmiths," Hans said as he primed one of our long rifles and handed it to me.

I sat down my load and took the rifle, cocked it, and sighted in on a French officer directing the fire of a cannon in the woods. I guessed him to be further than the two-hundred-fifty yards we tested our guns at. I wasn't sure I could hit him let alone hurt him. But what if I killed him?

A cannon ball exploded a section of wall fifty yards from me hurling two townsmen into the air, one a young lad.

French Bastards!

I took a deep breath, sighted a head high, released my air, and squeezed the trigger, just as ol' man MacDonald had taught me so long ago.

The officer seemed to drop into his boots.

The men and boys behind our wall cheered.

My stomach churned as I took a needed breath. "A head high," I said to Hans who nodded. He took my empty weapon and handed me another.

Hans showed a boy how to load the spent musket and set him to work as we emptied rifles into the artillerymen. Twenty shots later, fifteen of the French cannoneers were down. The enemy began moving the cannons deeper into the woods out of range and out of sight. The artillery was done.

Next we sighted in on the catapult operators. And a dozen shots later, the French pulled them back.

Without the support of the French, the Indians pulled back and the battle was over.

The townspeople gathered their wounded and dead.

Hans and I stood by the wagon surrounded by cheering men and boys.

Lotte rode around the house leading Rosey and stopped at the back of the celebrating crowd.

Though all the killing had sickened me, I helped Hans climb onto the bed of his wagon. He began handing out bags of powder and shot to the defenders of the wall.

I stood by the wagon fighting to retain my stomach contents.

The cheering continued until Hans raised a hand. "Gentlemen, please, we are not the heroes here today. You, the ones who took on overwhelming odds, you are the heroes."

"Hans, I've heard stories about your gun," said an older man with a white beard. "I've been in the gun making business for over twenty years, and I have never seen any weapon like the one you have created. That musket is unbelievable."

Hans, head nodding and blinking back emotions, dropped to knee and grabbed my shoulder with one of his ape-like arms. "I could not have made it without the wisdom and knowledge of this young man."

Lotte sitting on her horse, burst into tears.

I was close to joining her.

Hans stood. "We all need to get to the fort now, before these French and Indians decide to attack again; for they will."

Chapter Sixty-Eight

Hans drove his wagon now laden with the wounded sitting and laying on top of his store of arms through the empty streets of Lancaster Town. Despite the failing light, the street lamps weren't lit and the homes were all dark. Everyone had gone to the fort.

Lotte and I followed behind him on horseback.

The defenders of the wall trailed behind, a few riding, most walking.

Shortly after starting the trek, Hans stopped. He summoned the men and boys who were on horseback forward.

He glanced up at the darkening sky. "It will soon be night. And because of the wounded and the walking, we cannot travel very fast. Ye with horses need to go on to the fort and tell them we are coming, but we will not be there until after dark. And gentlemen, if you take my daughter with you and make sure she gets to the fort, I will be eternally in your debt."

I turned to Lotte. "Lotte, please listen to your father."

"And what are you going to do?" she asked.

"I'll give Rosey to one of the straggling walkers, and ride with your father. Just make sure Rosey is attended to when you get to the fort."

She grabbed my arm. "I've got a better idea, I'll ride with Pa and you walk. That way we'll take care of two of the stragglers or two of the wounded who can ride."

"None of these men are pregnant with my baby," I said quietly just for her to hear. Then in full voice, I said, "You *are* riding to the fort with these men."

"If I have to tie you to the horse," Hans added, looking up at her with stern eyes.

Lotte gave both Hans and I the same disgruntled look. Then she jerked her horse into line with the riders.

I gave Rosey to a young boy who had been walking.

I climbed aboard with Hans, and we rolled onward as the riders galloped out of sight.

Hans held his team of horses to a fast walk to ease the ride for the many wounded men in his wagon. There had to be at least a dozen men and boys wedged together.

It seemed like the riders whom we had sent ahead with Lotte had been gone forever, and yet we hadn't traveled very far.

I turned, gently helping a few of the wounded to move, and pulled a couple of our muskets off the stack of guns.

"What are you doing?" Hans asked.

"At the speed we're going, if the Indians are chasing us they'll catch us before we get to the fort. In the dark, we won't stand a chance."

He reached out and clutched my arm. "You're right, Hamish, but let someone else do whatever you are thinking." Then he leaned closer, "You need to start thinking like a man soon to be a father," he whispered, "not a frontiersman."

I had to look away from his imploring eyes to answer. "I know they're coming. I can feel it. Someone needs to slow them down so the rest of you can get to the fort."

He squeezed my arm, pulling my eyes back to him. "You are probably right. Those savages are coming. If I were them, I would. But going off in the dark by yourself to stop them is insane. They are night fighters and damned good ones. What do you know about fighting in the dark? You are not a wilderness animal like them. I doubt if you would detain them at all. You would be just wasting your life."

"But—"

"If you want to do something, get the two pistols I packed for you out of your chest. Then get off the wagon and put one of the slow boys in your place. Move half of the walkers in front of the wagon and the other half behind. And make them run. Then I'll pick up my speed to match theirs." He glanced skyward. "There is a sliver of moon, just enough to see the outline of the buildings lining the street."

I nodded. He was right. I swallowed my pride though the fear remained. Then I reached behind me and dug the two pistols out of the wooden chest. The thought that he had given me his personal pistols with his initials carved in them made my eyes water. I had hurt him so and yet he still couldn't hide his love.

I slung my rifle over my shoulder, stuffed the pistols in my pockets, and jumped off the wagon.

I placed the young men in front and the older men behind the wagon. And I challenged the young ones to out run the old men. And off we went into the night.

I fell to the rear hoping to detect the enemy before they caught us.

But if the Indians were close they had to hear thirty or more men running.

I slid to a stop and turned to face the darkness behind me, letting the noise of the clopping townsmen fade.

I listened and all I could hear was my heart thumping in my ears. And yet the hair on my arms and neck bristled.

They were coming. I sensed it.

Then I heard what I thought was soft patting of the dirt, like a bunch of children running.

I cocked the pistol. The click seemed so loud. Whatever noises I heard behind slowed and stopped.

Teeth chattering, I turned and sprinted toward Hans and hope.

Again the soft ground pounded behind me; getting closer.

Hans and the fleeing townspeople must be warned. I half-turned and fired the pistol into the blackness.

An arrow thudded into the dirt road a step or two away. Then several more shafts whizzed by me.

I ran harder, faster than I thought I could run. I kept up this out of control speed for what seemed to be easily far enough to have heard the heavy feet of the townspeople.

I should have caught them by now.

A few strides later, my nerves convinced me that something must have happened to Hans and his party. Maybe I should stop running and try to hide in one of these homes. Something was wrong.

I feared being stuck out here alone, so I kept going. And then in the dim light I saw what looked to be Hans' wagon turned blocking the street.

Many musket hammers cocked.

"Hold your fire!" Hans yelled in a harsh whisper. "Hamish, is that you?"

"Ay," I said. "And many Indians are close behind."

"Get behind the wagon, Lad," Hamish said.

As I ran around the end of the wagon, I detected many redcoats. The British soldiers were lined up four rows deep, each row the breadth of the street, standing behind the wagon.

Not knowing what else to do, I shouldered my musket and knelt down by the wagon tongue, where I found Hans.

Hans wrapped an arm around me. "Great to see you, Laddie. Half the fort must have come for us. and—"

"First row, at ready," a voice I didn't know softly commanded.

The noise of hundreds of light feet running toward us got louder and louder, until a dark mass could be seen approaching.

"Fire!" the voice commanded and the entire row shot their guns. The flashes of light briefly lit the night as the too-close-thunderclaps made me duck, frightening and yet reassuring.

"First row squat; reload. Second row, fire!"

Another horrific explosion of muskets boomed over top of us.

"Second row squat; reload. Third row fire!"

The bone jarring booms were deafening.

"Third row down and load. Fourth row fire."

Covering my ears did not stop the flinching jolt from the blasts immediately behind and above me.

"First row stand and fire!"

Another roar bounced off the street-lining buildings.

There could be no one left alive on the street in front of us. This had to be a slaughter.

Though my life had been saved, I felt no joy, only a numbing sadness.

"Second row stand at ready," the voice commanded. "Sargeant, send a few men to check on Platoons One and Two. I sent them to the streets east and west of us. They were to make sure we're not being flanked."

The battle was over.

I stood and peered around the end of the wagon. In the dark, gunsmoke-filled night, all I could see were forms on the ground, many forms; some moaning.

I prayed Papunuck wasn't among them.

Hans grabbed my hand and pulled himself up to his feet. "Help me hitch the horses and turn this wagon around. We need to go to the fort and find Lotte." Then he stopped and stepped in front of me. A smile creased his tear wetted face as he clasped both my arms. "And what say ye to finding a minister to make this family complete?"

"Aye." But this street of death wouldn't let me embrace his gracious offer. "Can the three of us leave this hate-filled place then?"

Chapter Sixty-Nine

Three months later

January, 1757

Late afternoon

I had just come into the house from the shop, shivering from the cold walk.

Lotte, her belly slightly bulged, stood over the hearth cooking.

"Good day, Mrs. MacCardle," I said, briskly stepping to her and the warmth of the fire. I took her into my arms and kissed her cheek.

She looked up at me. "I am so proud of my new name. Now all I need is for you to teach me is how to speak with your brogue."

I laughed. "Never. I want to show off my Dutch wife. A woman who can write and speak four languages and is a cello virtuoso."

She teasingly slapped my arm "You left off my greatest skill."

"And what may that be?" I asked thinking I knew her so well.

"That I am the best shot in Lancaster Town, maybe the Province of Pennsylvania." She grinned, drilling deep dimples in both cheeks.

"Someday, your pa and I must test that," I said.

"You may want to reconsider testing me." Her smirk was even lovely.

"Why?" I asked.

"Your pride may not recover from being beaten. And once beaten, you must forever live with my prowess . . . for I *will* remind you." She chuckled as she tapped my chest.

I smother her laughter with a kiss. Her lips were so warm and soft. Every time I kissed her it always seemed as exciting as the first time; a heart-racing, breath-taking enchantment.

She ended the long kiss, easing back to arms' length. "Hamish, I," she shook her head, "you make me so happy, and Pa as well. I haven't seen him this spry since you first came. I love you so. I know I tell you that every day. I pray you don't tire of it." She lurched back, her hand diving to her extended abdomen. "Oh."

"What?" I took a panicked step toward her.

She grabbed my hand and placed it on her bump.

Her belly fluttered against my palm. I gasped. This was the first time I had experienced feeling the life we'd created together. My joy burst forth in a smile and watery eyes. "Oh my God, the baby . . . to think that you and I have made a life. It's . . . it's unbelievable. And please tell me every day you love me. I live to hear it. I have been so fortunate to have come all this way and found you . . . you and your pa . . . and this little one whatever it may be; boy or girl. I'm truly blessed."

She took my hand and squeezed it. "We all are." Then she stepped back to the hearth. "Now I must finish cooking dinner." She stirred a pot. "Speaking of Pa, shouldn't he be back from the fort by now?"

"It took us most of the day yesterday to load his wagon. We practically emptied the shop except for some of our muskets yet to be delivered to the locals. He had his whole armory to negotiate and hopefully unload. I'd think he'd be awhile."

"I cannot believe Pa is actually going to leave Lancaster Town and go to Boston."

"As soon as he can sell this place," I said. "Like me, he doesn't want either you or the baby in this area during this war. And according to the people here from Boston, you should be able to at least get musical tutoring in Boston."

"But his business, he—"

"We can make and sell our guns anywhere in British America. The word has spread. We have orders from both New York and Boston."

She added chunks of sliced venison to the pot.

I leaned in and took a whiff. "Hmmm. That smells tasty."

She pushed me aside just as Hans came in the back door, a bulging bag flung over his shoulder. His nose and cheeks red from the cold.

"Lad, what are you doing here?" His eyebrows raised. "I thought you were going to finish those two muskets for the Jamisons."

"They are done, Sir."

"You never cease to amaze me, son." He smiled. "Your efforts top off a great day for us." He sat the bag down with a heavy clunk on a chair. "Mighty cold out there today." He blew on his hands. Then he shrugged out of his long, heavy coat, remove his hat and scarf, and stepped next to us in front of the fireplace, warming his hands.

Lotte stopped stirring. "Why a great day, Pa, what happened?"

Hans shook his head. "You are not going to believe what happened?"

"What?" I asked.

"Colonel Conrad Weiser, the commander of all the British militia in the Province of Pennsylvania and my friend . . . well, his wife recently had twins. They now have four children."

"Good for him," Lotte said. "Did you tell him you would soon be a grandfather?'

"Most certainly." Hans spread his arms.

"You weren't sure when you left, did he buy everything you took?" I asked.

Hans nodded, pointing at the bag and smiling. "Oh yes, everything."

"That's fantastic," I slapped my hands together.

"But there is more," Hans said. "The Colonel and his family have been relocated from Reading to Lancaster."

"Oh, to think that you would never have to make those trips anymore if we were staying here." Lotte's expression changed from happiness to concern. "We are still leaving, aren't we?"

Hans nodded his head. "Oh, yes."

I exchanged a bewildered look with Lotte. "That's the 'there is more'?" I asked.

"No. I saved the best until the end." He grinned. "There are not accommodations large enough at the fort for a man of his rank with that large of a family." Hans slowly sat down, beaming a smile. "To reward him for his excellent service record in the British America, the British Government has given him both the permission as well as the funds to buy our place."

Chapter Seventy

Two weeks later

At first light, we were a sullen group bundled up in winter garb. The surrounding brown grass was a frost-covered gray. A slight wind deepened the cold.

I helped Lotte up on a wagon, sitting her on a blanket-covered seat. I placed a bag of hot stones by her feet, and then tucked the blanket around her feet, legs, and torso. "That should warm you in a few minutes."

Hans climbed onto a second large vehicle. "With all the sunshine we have had for the past week, the road should be free of snow. A good day to travel."

It was very hard for me to again say good-bye to the Blekkink's property. The stone-home, our fort, in which I had discovered love and my new family. The shop where I had spent so many wonderful and creative hours with Hans. And the barn where me, a city boy, had grown to love a horse, and Rosey had in turn showed me her trust and affection.

I walked around the wagon making sure everything was secure. Along the way I gave a pat to Rosey, tied to the rear with Lotte's horse.

Hans had been quiet all day yesterday as we packed his two new Conestoga wagons with all of our personal items, furniture, shop tools, and provisions. I could sense his struggle with leaving his beautiful home and workshop he had built and the grounds in which he had buried his wife.

And despite Lotte's happiness about getting out of the war, she had cried herself to sleep last night in my arms.

I waited for Hans' lead.

He stood and gazed around for a long moment and then sat, also covering his legs with a blanket. He shouted a command to the four-horse team and rolled away.

I slapped the reins on the lead team's backs, and we rolled away behind Hans.

When the sun had just cleared the horizon, our two wagons were rolling out of Lancaster Town, following eight soldiers, a stagecoach with four passengers driven by Frank, and trailed by eight more redcoats.

As we rolled away from the town into the rolling tree-covered hills, all my fears and anxieties of the wilderness returned. My head began turning, eyes scanning. My shoulder muscles tightened in anticipation of the danger sure to come. Despite the invading January cold air, sweat trickled down my spine and my glove-covered palms were wet.

I shrugged, hoping to dispel my fears. I glanced at Lotte, hoping she hadn't noticed my condition.

Lotte, head bowed, eyes closed, and hands squeezing the blanket around her, was praying.

I waited until she sat upright. "What are you praying for?"

"That we get to Philadelphia without anyone getting hurt."

"We'll be fine," I said with as much confidence as I could muster.

"You need to save that song for those who haven't danced to it before," she said, staring at me and then flicking a bead of sweat off my forehead. "You're already sweating, and it's freezing out here."

"I have too many clothes on."

"Hamish, we're in Indian country."

"Ay." I tapped the wooden seat with my knuckles. "Hans made sure both of these wagons were made with high sides of four-inch-thick wood. They both are rolling forts. And we have twenty of our new muskets in here, all loaded. There is room for all of us, the soldiers, the coach passengers, and us in these two forts."

"But the French have cannons," she said.

"Given enough warning, we can outrun the French cannons," I said.

"But not the Indians." Her expression voiced concern.

Taking the four reins in one hand, I reached out and patted her blanket-covered hand. "We'll do what we have to do. We're all experienced. There is no need to worry."

"I pray so," she said. "I just don't want anything to—"

"Shhh," I leaned over and kissed her cheek. "Besides, I have nothing to fear, I'm sitting next to the best shot in the Province of Pennsylvania."

One of her arms came out of her shroud, picked up the musket wedged in the foot trough, and placed it across her lap. "I hope I don't have to prove that to you on this trip."

"We'll be fine."

Chapter Seventy-One

Shortly after mid-day, we stopped at a creek. Two of the soldiers rode on to check out the tree-covered road as it rose into the nearby hills.

With some of the redcoats volunteering to water the horses, Hans and Frank walked up to us.

"We are close to Exton, a small hamlet of ten or fifteen homes," Frank said. "There is no inn. We will build a fire and eat there using our own provisions. Then we will push on from there to Reesville, where we will stay the night. And then tomorrow we should be in Philadelphia sometime after mid-day."

"I pray the flag is up in Reesville," I said.

"What?" Hans asked.

Frank laughed at me. "Hamish and I first became acquainted at Reesville. Another one of my many stories. It's a shame Charlie isn't here to tell it. He was a great story-teller."

Lotte grabbed my arm. "Tell us, Frank, there is so much I don't know about Hamish," Lotte said.

"It was nothing," I said. "My first frightening experience with the wilderness; but, thank God, nothing happened."

Frank looked at Lotte, grinned, and nodded.

"It's so cold," Lotte said, hugging herself.

I stepped over and pulled her inside my coat.

She looked up at me. "Is that where you first saw Papunuck?"

I shook my head.

"Who?" Frank asked.

"Just another story, Frank," I said.

He shrugged. "It's cold, but it's the best time of year to make this trip. All the leaves are off the trees. The woods are clear. Which makes it a more difficult place for the Indians to surprise us. Also in the clearings either the frost or the snow shows all tracks. If anyone has recently been in the area, we will know it. I have seen no traces of anyone since we left Lancaster Town."

I could feel Frank's words ease the tension in Lotte's body.

Bless him.

And though I trusted him, I knew I wouldn't be comfortable until we were in Philadelphia.

Chapter Seventy-Two

The inhabitants of Reesville amazed me. So few living in the middle of madness. I wondered how they could sleep at night? Why were they here on this hilltop in the middle of nowhere? And yet they were all so joyful. Each pulling as much news from us as possible about us, Lancaster Town, and the war.

After a warm dinner, it started to snow. The redcoats graciously volunteered to cover all of the four-hour night watches. The rest of us settled in the barn. Though the fresh straw the locals put down was nice, the barn was not much warmer than outside and smelled like horses. And the twenty of us took up most of the available space.

Lotte, Hans, and I settled in a corner where despite the darkness, we pushed straw into the gaps in the wall boards. Then we snuggled together under our blankets.

"Our last night in the wilderness, thank God," Hans said in a hushed voice to not disturb the others.

"You must be sad, I think we all are," I said softly. "You had such a beautiful place in Lancaster Town."

"The war robbed it of its beauty," Hans said. "Actually, I am excited about starting over in Boston. I have so many ideas of how to improve both our home and a shop."

"A new home with a baby's room," Lotte added, wiggling against me.

"Ay," I said.

"The warmest, best room in the house," Hans said.

"We will set up a shop where we can build our guns faster and more accurate than anyone else," I said.

"Ay," Hans added with a light chuckle. "So what will we call this child?"

"Hamish and I have already decided," Lotte whispered. She squeezed my arm. "Hans if a boy, and Mary, after Hamish's mother, if a girl."

"Hans if a boy," Hans paused, "Hans MacCardle, sounds different but makes me proud. Now Mary MacCardle flows like Lotte's cello music. I like them both."

"Thank you," I said, patting his shoulder. "Time to get some rest, I'm going to spell one of those redcoats for sentry duty in a few hours."

"Hamish no, it's cold and dangerous. And who will keep me warm?" Lotte asked.

"It's only fair, I along with one of the coach passengers have committed to take one of the watches." I hugged her. "It's only a few hours."

"Let me do that in your stead," Hans said.

"That is kind of you to offer, but it would be too hard on your leg," I replied. "I'll have both my pistols and my musket and my long warm coat; all thanks to you. I'll be fine. Now let's us sleep."

Chapter Seventy-Three

Chilled from leaving Lotte's warmth, I stepped from the barn greeted by a steam cloud of my breath and snow falling.

The half-moon provided enough light to create shadows on the ground from the surrounding buildings and trees. The new snow crunched under my boots as I along with one of the male coach passengers and two soldiers met the four soldiers who had been on guard duty. Each of the retiring men pointed to the position they had left.

I was directed to a lookout spot where the trail left Reesville toward Philadelphia, overlooking the vast meadow in the valley below. I remembered this meadow as if it were yesterday. This is where I had tasted my first fear of the wilderness. Our coach had stopped awaiting the raising of an all-is-safe flag in Reesville. The memory caused a small shudder to coarse through me.

I stood in the shadow of the trees to be concealed from the light breeze as well as from anyone trying to enter the village.

It didn't take me long to regret volunteering. The cold bit at my fingers and the tips of my ears. Every sound became a potential threat. By myself in the dark, four hours would seem like a lifetime.

Every now and then I would move from one tree to another to keep my feet warm.

It was so quiet at one point I was sure I could hear the snow pelting the ground. Next I thought I saw movement in the valley. After straining my eyes, I convinced myself my imagination was playing games with my senses. I moved back to the place where I had entered the sparse woods. I leaned against a tree and took several deep breaths, trying to relax. Though I smelled something strange, I pushed it aside, not trusting my fear-tainted senses.

I didn't know if I finally got used to the cold, or if I was too numb to feel it. But eventually, my control returned as the black chill surrounding me became a quiet dark blanket.

I let my mind wander, thinking of what Lotte's and my baby would look like. It was one of my favorite things to do when I was alone with time on my hands. Hopefully, if the baby were a girl, she would have Lotte's features and pale blue eyes. And if a boy, he would have Hans' strength and wisdom, and my height and my mother's heart.

My thoughts of how our baby would look helped take my mind off my stinging ears, nose, hands and feet. I sat down in a low fork of a branch and leaned against the tree trunk and let my heavy eyelids close——I bolted upright. How long had I been asleep? I blinked and looked around into the dark trees. Something had awakened me. I shook the cold from my head, and saw the ground at my feet. There were footprints in the snow leading away from my perch. I fisted my musket and whipped my head around to scan my surroundings. Fear surged, as I cocked the musket and something, a small leather pouch, was hanging from the hammer. I stared at the curiously out of place object. Had my musket caught hold of something left hanging from a branch? No this had been placed on my gun. Chills raced from my scalp down my spine. No one was in sight and I still had my hair. I eased the soft bag off my gun and, concerned about what it contained, I squeezed it gently. The contents were soft and pliant. Obviously nothing alive or threatening.

Looking around one more time, I leaned my weapon against the tree and opened the bag, pouring the contents into my hand. There in the moonlight in my large hand were an expertly crafted pair of deer skin infant's moccasins.

Chapter Seventy-Four
May, 1757
Boston
Early morning

I was late for work. I'd spent too much time this sun-blessed morning making sure Lotte was feeling fine. By her count, the baby was due in the next three to four weeks. I think I was more excited than she was and much more nervous.

As I walked through the dirt-packed streets of Boston, cluttered with early risers, my thoughts focused on the baby to come. I hoped we were ready for the little person. With Hans' help I had made an infant's crib and a rocking chair Lotte could use to feed the baby.

I had hung the little moccasins on the corner of the baby's bed in anticipation of the day Lotte and I could put them on the newborn's feet.

When I had first shown Lotte the soft leather baby's slippers, she couldn't stop her tears. Papunuck was a good man. He was something rare, like a spring-fed water hole in the middle of a desert; both a savior and a life-long memory.

Having lived in the wilderness, people we met in Boston always wanted to know if we ever encountered any of the savages they had heard stories about. Lotte and I, and even Hans, loved to tell our Papunuck stories. Most of the Bostonians seemed both disappointed and shocked to be told Indians were just like us, human beings with hearts and souls.

I turned a corner onto the street where Hans had purchased an old warehouse which we had converted into a gun-making shop.

A young blond-headed boy, maybe ten-years-old, was peering through the opened door. I had frequently seen this young man over the past few weeks. His clothes were rags, he was barefoot, and looked as if he had never had a bath or a haircut.

He reminded me of the lad I once was, hanging around ol' MacDonald's shop, looking for work.

"Hey there, Laddie, what be your name?" I called out as I walked up behind him.

He glanced over his shoulder with large eyes and turned to leave.

I grabbed his arm. "Whoa there. I'm not going to hurt you. I just want to know your name."

He looked at my hand on his arm and then into my eyes, unsure of my intentions. "Johnny," he pulled his arm free, "Johnny Weidemann."

"I'm Hamish, Hamish MacCardle. I see you around here often, what interests you?"

He looked down. "Ah, ah the guns." His coal-black eyes returned to mine. "Yous make guns, doncha?"

"That we do, Johnny. We make what is known as the Blekkink Long Rifle, which is quite sought after in the colonies."

"Yous has to be really smart. I wish I could make a gun."

"Anyone can learn the basics, but to make something special does require a little science and some math skills."

He glanced away and shook his head. "I guess I just be dreamin', cause I'm not good with the numbers."

"You're just a kid. How old are you?"

"I'm eleven."

Hans stuck his head out of the door. "I have been listening to you two chattering out here. You are late, Mister MacCardle." Then he noticed the boy. "So I see you caught the little bugger. He has been hanging around here for weeks."

"Hans, meet Johnny Weidemann. Johnny this is Mister Blekkink. Johnny wants to be a gun maker."

"Does he now?" Hans eyed the boy. "He looks a might frail for hard work."

Johnny straightened his skinny frame. "Oh, I can work and work hard. Least ways that's what my pa used to tell me afore he . . . he left."

His words stung me like aggravated hornets. "Who do you live with, Johnny?"

"Me mum, and four brothers and sisters."

"Where did your pa go?" Hans asked.

"Mum says he's out west somewhere with the British Army. He sends a little money now and again."

I looked at Hans who was eyeing me. "What do you think, Partner? Do you think we could use a hand to clean up the shop and maybe run errands for us?"

Hans rubbed his chin as he looked the boy up and down. "Well, I guess we could give him a try and see if he can do the work. But he will need to know his numbers to become a gun maker. So he must go to school to learn math. Can you do that?" Hans asked the boy.

"All the schools here be private. I can't afford no schooling."

"Hmm," Hans said, shaking his head. "So if you went to school, do you think you could learn reading, writing, and arithmetic?"

"I think so. Me mum says I'm like my dad, and he's smart. He's a Sergeant in the British army."

"What do you think, Hamish?" Hans asked. "Do you think this boy is worth the investment of schooling and clothes, and a few meals?"

"The only way to find out is to give him a chance and test him now and then," I said. "Plus, just looking at him, I think he'll need a small salary to help feed his family."

The boy wrung his hands, shifting his weight from foot to foot. "I'll work real hard both in school and for you; you'll see."

Hans took a deep breath and released it. "We could use some help for sure." He rubbed his chin. "Maybe he could work for us in the afternoons for a few hours after school and all day on Saturdays. We'll pay for his schooling, his clothes, meals on Saturdays, and how about we start out at a half pound a month. What say you, Johnny?"

The boy's eyes grew large again and he jumped in the air. "A half pound per month and clothes and school. Yes! Ah, I mean yes, Sir. I'll study real hard in school, I promise. Can I start tomorrow? Me mum will be so happy."

Hans smiled and patted the small boy on the back. "We will see you tomorrow morning. Then Mr. MacCardle will take you to get some school and work clothes. Then he'll get you enrolled in a local school as soon as possible. After that you can start work."

"I'll be here." Johnny took off running like he was late for Christmas.

I stepped next to Hans. "Thank you, Hans. You have just made me and that boy's family very happy. Based on his appearance, his family is probably starving. We'll test the boy along the way and see if he's worth an apprenticeship."

"Just as Ol' man MacDonald did with another wee-lad many years ago, thank God."

I nodded and smiled.

I glanced over Hans' shoulder. The forge was hot. It was time to go to work.

The End

Author's Note:

Thank you for reading my novel. A 'comment' on Amazon at the book site would be greatly appreciated.

Please review the descriptions of my other published books listed on the next page. Perhaps you will find another story of mine that peaks your interest.

Respectfully,

Dave McDonald

Dave McDonald's Books:

"Kugi's Story"
"Dead Winners"
"Sam's Folly"
"Death Insurance"
"More Than A Game" by Mark Collins/Dave McDonald
"Too Many"
"A Common Uprising"
"Killing by Numbers"

Soon to be published:
"Mickey's Wars"

About the author:

A romanticist at heart, with a deductive mind, I am a graduate engineer who traveled the world keeping commercial jet engines flying safely.

I thought I loved my first career until I found my second, writing. In retrospect, my first profession incited me via information; the sights, smells, emotions, experiences, and stories for my second career.

I've written thirteen novels (ten either published or in process), with several more in seed.

I live with my wife, Linda, and dog, Bentley, on Hilton Head Island, South Carolina.

Made in the USA
Columbia, SC
16 November 2020